Clos

The I

Ben Westerham was born in 1964 in London. After many years spent writing in bits and pieces, Ben now primarily writes crime, mystery and thriller fiction, often with a healthy serving of humour. He lives in rural Northamptonshire in the English Midlands.

The House of Spies

BEN WESTERHAM

Published by Close9 Publishing

ISBN:978-1-911085-35-5

ALSO BY BEN WESTERHAM

BANBURY CROSS MURDER MYSTERY SERIES

The Hide and Seek Murders
The Club of Death
The Hobby Horse Murder
A Legacy of Death

DAVID GOOD PRIVATE INVESTIGATOR SERIES

Good Investigations
The Strawberry Girl
Good Girl Gone Bad
Too Good to Die
Smart Way to Die
The Good Con
Good and the Vanishing Act
As Good as Dead

SHORTS IN THE DARK SERIES

Collector of Crimes
Shattered Dreams

50FOR30 MICRO SHORTS SERIES

50for30 Series One
50for30 Series Two

MULTI-AUTHOR ANTHOLOGIES

Breakneck

DEDICATION

For Brenda Cartwright, mother, wife and grandmother, to whom we said goodbye this Autumn. Now gone but never forgotten.

It's all English to me

A word on the language that's used in this book, so you know what to expect. The version of English that is used here is British. This ought not to present much in the way of a problem for non-British readers. If you do find the occasional word or phrase a little odd, then I hope you still understand the essence of what is being said.

A JOURNEY NORTH

The story I am about to convey is one that I fear you, like any sane person, will find somewhat remarkable, perhaps even a little incredulous. I must make it clear, however, that it is, from beginning to end, entirely true, despite its most unusual nature.

It may, perhaps, remind you of some of those Boys Own adventures popular with the reading public for a good many years now, but I can assure you my tale is a faithful recounting, even if some of the more obscure details have become a little fuzzy with the passing of time.

Perhaps the years that have past and the momentous events that have occurred since my own modest adventure will make it a little easier for you, the reader, to accept the proposition that I present to you and not to think I am in possession of an unbalanced mind, capable of the most outrageous exaggerations.

As it is, I was for many years subject to the controls and strictures of His Majesty's Government that prohibited me from saying a single word about my experiences, the subject matter being one considered too sensitive for public consumption. Indeed, before we proceed any further, I wish to make it clear that I am grateful for the recent lifting of these restrictions, since I would not otherwise have been able to share this tale with you now.

My story is set seven years ago, in the spring of 1912, though it remains so fresh in my mind that it could be less than a single year since. I should add, for the avoidance of confusion and muddle, that I lived then, as I do now, in a plain little house in Pimlico, London, and was at that time a single man of modest means, sufficient to keep body and soul together and to enjoy the occasional minor extravagance.

*

I had intended to pay a visit to my godparents on the occasion of their thirty-second wedding anniversary. It had been some time since I had seen them and, what with their being at home for the weekend and my not being committed to some other, inconveniently timed, engagement, I eagerly sent word that I would be with them on the Friday evening. Their encouragement of my visit was most wholehearted, with only a mild rebuke for my previous and rather extended lack of attention.

I have always been thankful to my parents for their fine choice of John and Susan Buchan as my godparents since they have, at all times, undertaken the role wonderfully well and, if truth be told, they have rather spoiled me at every opportunity. Their one and only child, a son, George, is eleven years older than me, and has been living, since the age of twenty-one, in South Africa. I sometimes suspect that the attention they would otherwise have showered on him, had he remained in the country, they have instead directed towards me, seeing how I am rather more readily to hand.

Since my visit was to be for a single weekend, I packed just the one small suitcase and a heavy coat, which any sensible person considers an essential item for a trip to Scotland, even in the spring. I also took with me a small bottle of my godmother's favourite scent, Christiane, something by Guerlain, I recall. This my godmother finds frustratingly difficult to obtain in Scotland, it seemingly being unavailable anywhere outside of Edinburgh.

My little apartment in Warwick Square looked the picture of order and silent contentment as I picked up my coat and suitcase and stepped out into the cool, rather brightly-lit hallway. It was seven-thirty-eight in the evening and I was pleased to find myself seven minutes ahead of schedule; not something I am wholly accustomed to, since I am, on occasion, rather tardy where my time-keeping is concerned.

*

Euston railway station was rather quiet by normal standards. Nothing like the noisy, jostling crowds of people coming hither and thither that you find there earlier in the day and it made for rather a pleasant change; all the more so seeing how I had such a lengthy journey ahead of me. As there remained above an hour before my train was due to depart, I took temporary ownership of one of the tables at the dining rooms on platform six and ordered a strong coffee.

I picked up a copy of the afternoon's newspaper, intending to while away the time perusing its pages. But it was a hopeless case and I found myself unable to do more than cast a roving eye over the headlines. My problem was that familiar little thrill of excitement one gets when about to set off on a long and eagerly anticipated journey, which began to grow inside me the moment I entered the railway station, and I wondered if I should be able to sleep at all on the overnight express. I was once again a schoolboy, setting off on a journey to some distant location with my parents, bursting at the seams with excitement.

I was not, however, left free to enjoy this happy state of burgeoning excitement for long. Barely ten minutes after sitting down, there was a firm tap on my shoulder. I looked around, startled from my daydream.

"Alexander Templeman, as I live and breathe. It is you."

A familiar, round and somewhat blotchy face looked down at me, smiling broadly. It was one I had not seen for some years.

"George Latching. What a coincidence. How the devil are you?"

I jumped to my feet and we shook hands, both visibly delighted at such a fortunate and unexpected encounter.

"Can't complain. Well, I probably could, but I'd be nit-picking. You travelling north or waiting for someone to arrive?"

"Travelling a long way north, as it happens. Scotland. Take a seat and let me get you something to drink," I insisted, eager to catch up on old times.

"A cup of tea would do very nicely."

George and I had attended the same school, Braunston Hall in Withering Dean, and although I'd kept in touch with a good number of the old boys, I'd not seen George for several years, after he'd moved to Nottingham to take up a position in the family firm. They were lace-makers and, I recalled, he was the fifth generation to take on the responsibility of managing the business. He'd put on a little weight, it seemed to me, his cheeks rather fuller than I remembered and his midriff perhaps somewhat more rounded. I wondered if I'd changed much myself, though found it hard to believe that I had.

The minutes flew by as we spoke eagerly about our school days, re-acquainting ourselves with friends and enemies, and revisiting deeds both happy and infamous. I found it hard to believe that my school days were already so far behind me, although I suppose eight years is not really a very great deal of time, in the great scheme of things.

Almost before we knew it, the time came for George to board the Nottingham-bound train and we shook hands warmly, having exchanged addresses and earnestly promised to visit each other at the first possible opportunity. As his train began to pull away, I looked again at my watch. There were only ten minutes remaining until my own was scheduled to depart. I picked up my bag, paid the bill and, with an added spring in my step after such a fortuitous meeting, boarded the Euston to Glasgow overnight express and made my way to my compartment.

It was a pleasantly warm evening, one that presented London at something of its best. The soft amber light of the setting sun had cast a most pleasing glow over the buildings I passed on my way to the station and the air retained just sufficient warmth to keep off a chill. I doubt I could have asked for a more pleasing evening for my departure.

Precisely on time, the train began to pull out of the station, crawling through a vast, swirling cloud of smoke, the wheels squealing as they bit against the steel rails. A handful of well-wishers waved off loved ones and, for a moment, I felt a pang of sadness as I was myself leaving someone behind. I had said farewell that afternoon to Caroline Carsons, to whom I hoped soon to become engaged, with a promise to return with one of Scotland's finest tartan scarves as a present. Although not altogether convinced myself that it passed muster as a suitable gift, Caroline was adamant that was what she wanted and who was I to argue? Now, alone, with no one to wave me off, I re-affirmed my determination to speak to Caroline's father about my desire to marry his daughter. It would be my most urgent business upon my return to London.

*

The train made good time and I retired to my compartment and bed a little before eleven, after enjoying a late supper and a glass or two of whiskey in the company of two most entertaining men of business, who were to alight at Rugby. So agreeable was their company that I rather regretted the fact they would not be there to talk to over an early breakfast in the buffet car.

I slept well, not being someone who finds their sleep interrupted by overnight travel, and, as a result, awakened early enough to be one of the first to be seated for breakfast. It's a meal I never miss, not if I can help it. A good breakfast sets you up for the day, I do believe, and I'd rather forgo luncheon and dinner if I could have only the one meal in the course of a day.

By then we were already steaming through the open countryside north of Carlisle, so I returned to my compartment and packed away my few things ready for our arrival in Glasgow, my anticipation at staying with my godparents growing once again now that the longer leg of my journey was approaching its end. We pulled into the station at eight-fourteen, a mere four minutes late and a very commendable effort given the distance we had travelled.

As anyone who has been there could tell you, Glasgow Central station is large and impressive, considerable rebuilding work having been completed only as recently as 1905, and it was thronging with people setting about their daily business, a great cacophony of sound filling my ears as I stepped off the train. It might have been pleasant to linger a while to study the architecture, but I had little time for such luxuries as my connecting train departed only eleven minutes later and I had first to ascertain which platform I needed to make my way to.

After a near miss, which would have seen me boarding

a train to the west coast, I found myself staring out the window of a local service as it pulled slowly out of the station. Before long, we were passing through the town of Kilmarnock, having already called at several smaller halts, and heading towards the stop at which I would alight, in the hamlet of New Cumnock.

As I gazed once more at the outside world, the green and brown hues that had predominated since we left Glasgow began to dissipate and, in places, disappear into a shifting whitewash of thickening cloud. It seemed a heavy spring fog was moving in from the sea, only a handful of miles away to the west. I ran a hand over my coat as it lay across my lap, thankful I had not succumbed to the temptation to think the weather during my stay might be only ever fine. I did, however, wonder how difficult a proposition it would be for me to locate my godparents' rather isolated house in the thickening fog. How embarrassing it would be for me if they should find it necessary to send out a search party to rescue me, if I ended up wandering aimlessly in the fog.

LOST IN A GREAT FOG

New Cumnock is a village, a small one at that, and the railway station nothing more than a minor halt with a modest ticket office; but rarely can a sight have been more welcome, for it was my final stop. I was the only passenger to alight there and none, as far as I could see, boarded the southbound train.

I was greeted by almost complete silence, the still thickening fog nullifying any sounds that may have been there in the background. It was also distinctly chilly and I buttoned up my coat before making my way towards the ticket office, where the station master had some unwelcome news. The bus I had intended should take me most of the way to the house was out of service and a replacement was not available.

Ordinarily, my godfather would have met me at the station with his horse and buggy, but he was away on business, I knew, and not due back until later in the day. It seemed I faced the disconcerting prospect of having to make my way to the house on foot; a relatively easy enough task for someone like me with at least a basic knowledge of the area, but an altogether different matter in the thickening mass of white cloud.

The station master must have sensed my concern because I had not long stepped out on to the street and begun to steel myself for this last, unexpectedly challenging leg of my journey when he reappeared at my side. He informed me that a farm labourer with a horse-drawn cart, who had just dropped off some supplies at the station, had other stops to make and, if I cared to offer him a modest payment for his troubles, was willing to make a detour to my godparents' house. The man also knew where this was located, so would have no need for me to make an attempt at providing directions.

There was something about the way the station master conveyed this news that I should have taken more notice of, but I was all too happy to accept the offer and made no attempt to identify what it was that lay behind the slight sense of reticence I detected. It seemed I had enjoyed a considerable degree of good fortune, since, if I had arrived in the village only a few minutes later, the farm labourer and his cart would have already departed.

*

The farm labourer, who went by the name of Fraser Brooke, was a surly looking fellow with a large, unkempt beard and eyes that shifted around disconcertingly, as if he never wanted to linger on anything or anyone for very long, and he had the most enormous hands I believe I'd ever seen.

As I clambered up on to the cart and took up station next to him, his stale, alcohol-laced breath took me by surprise and I had to turn my head away for a moment to recover. I suspected at once what had lain behind that sense of unease I'd noticed on the part of the station master, who had already made his way back to his office. I supposed beggars were not to be choosers and attempted to engage my new associate in conversation, but what few words he uttered in reply were barely comprehensible and I decided it was best thereafter to let him concentrate on his driving.

As we clattered away from the station, past several stone-built cottages that were typical in appearance of those in the region, I couldn't help but notice the fog had now become so thick that I doubted we could see more than twenty yards in front of us. My sense of relief at finding someone to take me to the house grew more certain. By now, I wasn't sure I'd even be able to find my own way out of the village, let alone to the road that would take me to my godparents. I tugged at my coat lapels, so as to bring them closer about my cheeks and sunk my head down into my shoulders, all the better to keep out the growing chill.

After twenty minutes or so, we turned off the main road and on to a bumpy dirt and stone track, over which the small, brown horse struggled for sure footing. It led us up a shallow incline, to a tumbledown farmhouse, where my still largely silent driver jumped off, hauled a sack of some unseen supplies from the back of the cart, and dropped it at the feet of the old woman who came to the door in response to his loud, heavy knock. He appeared to expend as few words on her as he had on me, which made me feel a little less unwelcome than I had up until that point.

We called at two further cottages after that, though quite where they were in relation to each other was hard to say, since I was by now completely befuddled by the fog which, it seemed to me, was already looking well set for a lengthy stay, with no whisper of a breeze to blow it away. It was as we left the first of these two cottages that I found it necessary to reproach my driver for the first time, though little good it did me. Before moving away, he pulled a small flask from an inner pocket of his heavy, leather jacket, unscrewed the lid and took a hearty draw on the contents. The smell left me in no doubt that it was alcohol he was drinking. Whiskey seemed most likely, given that we were in Scotland. Since he was obviously already under the influence and our journey was a hazardous one, I felt I couldn't let this incident go unchallenged and suggested to the man that he ought to save his drink for the end of the day.

Rather than heed my practical advice, he looked at me for a time, his eyes brooding under dark, bushy brows, took another drink from his flask, then made himself very clear. "You can always take to your feet if you no like my company."

The sudden and unexpected clarity of his speech caught me off balance and I dithered as to a response. He had the upper hand, after all, and I realised I stood little chance of finding my own way back to the village, let alone my godparents' house, so I offered no resistance and we made our way back to the road in what was by now our customary silence.

I have no idea how far we had travelled, but I do know almost an hour had elapsed since we had left the railway station, and I supposed we could not have gone particularly far from the village as a result of our slow speed and the several stops. All the same, I began to grow increasingly restless for our arrival at Hillside House. My driver had resorted to his flask several times more since our last stop and was by now humming some odd, erratic tune I could not make out as we swayed from side-to-side, the reins light in his large, dirty hands. I must admit to some concern that he might, in fact, have no idea as to our whereabouts, nor give a care in the world about his passenger.

We had crested a gentle rise, where my hope of finding a break in the fog proved to be forlorn, then began to descend the other side. As we did so, my driver seemed content to let the horse pick up a little speed and you could almost say we ran on at a trot, despite the limited visibility, which caused me to grip with both hands the wooden bench on which we were seated.

I cannot be altogether sure of what happened next, but my recollection is that an animal of some sort, a fox perhaps, ran out in front of us, causing the horse to take fright. I supposed the poor horse must have been taken aback at the sudden appearance of this wild animal, whatever it was, and, spooked in the extreme, bolted forward without hesitation or warning. It was fortunate indeed that I was holding on to the seat, because I suspect that otherwise I would have been thrown clear and no doubt risked injury in landing on the uneven track.

Worse still, my driver allowed the reins to slip through his hands, no doubt a situation not helped by his inebriated condition, and, as he struggled to steady himself, groped ineffectually down by his feet in search of the reins.

"Good God, man," I shouted, fear beginning to take command of me. "Take hold of those reins again before we're hopelessly out of control."

There was some mumbled reply that I could not make out, but already I was aware our speed was continuing to build and our path growing ever more erratic, as out of the fog a low stone wall loomed at my side of the cart before shrinking back into the cloud as we surged first to one side and then the other, leaving me desperately struggling to keep my seat.

"Slow, yer bugger," came the command from my right, but the horse paid no heed.

My heart was now racing and my breathing rapid, every muscle in my body tensed for a sudden, violent impact. Deep, guttural oaths began to rain down on the terrified horse from its owner, who, I noticed, had by some miracle managed to lay one hand on the reins. But, at the very moment it seemed salvation was at hand, there was an especially violent lurch to the right. The world became a confused, swirling mass of blurred images, all blending one into another and a cacophony of screaming, grating sounds filled my ears.

*

I opened my right eye, a little at first, then fully, and saw… nothing. All was white; an odd, soft white that seemed not to be solid, but shifting, almost imperceptibly. For a while, as I stared into this void, I had absolutely no idea where I was or why, nor even, for that matter, who I was. It was a truly peculiar sensation; one that, I admit now with some embarrassment, caused me to think that perhaps I had left behind my earthly life and passed on into another realm. Though why that might have happened I could not explain.

Before I could develop these thoughts further, reality began to push in on me. My head was first to make itself known, with a terrible, throbbing pain that caused me to wince in discomfort, so much so that I felt nauseous. As I struggled to come to terms with my aching head, I became aware that the whole of my right side was cold and damp and, as I turned my head with care a little to the side, I realised I was lying on the ground. It was then that my memories came flooding back and I realised that the farm cart I had been travelling in had overturned, sending me crashing against the stone wall I had stared down on with such horror only moments before. The all-consuming whiteness into which I faced was the fog that had slowly but surely engulfed us since we left the railway station; it seemed undiminished by the passing of time.

That thought made me wonder how long I had been lying there in the road. Taking care, least I might have suffered further as yet unannounced injuries, I reached inside my jacket with my left hand, searching for my pocket watch. Having located it and lifted it into view, I brought my eyes to focus on its face. It was ten thirty-three. I had been unconscious for something like ten minutes, probably a little less. My head throbbed yet more at the effort required to focus and when I tested the most sensitive area with the fingers of one hand they came back sticky, coated with a thin layer of partially-congealed blood.

First checking my battered body for broken limbs or other serious injuries – of which there seemed to be none, thank God – I eased myself inch by painful inch back on to my feet, so unsteady at first that I had to reach out a hand to purchase support against the very wall that had done me damage. I stood for a moment and listened; the silence was total. The fog seemed to be even thicker than it was before we had crashed, visibility now little more than ten feet at best, or so I guessed.

As I stood there, nausea returned and I had to lean bodily against the dulled, damp edges of the stone wall for further support. It took some little while for the sensation to pass, whereupon I began to consider my situation.

In other circumstances, where the expectation of being found by some passing stranger might have been greater, I would have stayed where I was and waited for assistance, but there seemed so little likelihood of such an event, in so remote a place, that I made my mind up I would have to find my own way to some sort of help. A farmhouse, perhaps.

Rather than wander off aimlessly, I thought it best to first attempt to locate the farm labourer and the horse and cart, which I hoped to find intact, though it seemed somewhat unlikely. Still feeling groggy and uncertain on my feet, I staggered with care into the fog, not sure whether I was returning the way we had come or heading in the opposite direction; not that it seemed to make much difference. So slow was my progress that a child only recently able to walk would probably have passed me by with ease, but it was, for the time being, all I could manage.

I had made my painful way for perhaps two hundred yards, when I began to make out a blurred, possibly rectangular, shape in the fog ahead of me. As I closed a little further, I was able to see that it was the cart, now lying on one side, its contents spilled across the track. Perhaps the farm labourer had faired better than me in the crash and, seeing me lying there unconscious, gone off in search of help. If that appeared to be the case, I would change my plan and wait there for my rescuers to arrive.

Such hopes were, however, entirely dashed almost as soon as they arose. Barely had I reached the nearest end of the cart than I made out the form of a man sprawled upon the ground on the other side of the track, his face towards the sky. As I closed in on him, I began to fear the worst. His left arm was twisted underneath his body in a hideously unnatural position and a large pool of blood stained the ground around his head. I knelt down next to him and did my best to find a pulse, first at a temple, then on a wrist, but there appeared to be none. His eyes, when I lifted the lids, showed no signs of life. It did not escape my attention that, but for the grace of God, it could have been me lying there dead and the labourer searching for signs of life.

As I stood up, I noticed a face looking at me from out of the fog, only a few yards away. If the horse was feeling any sense of blame for what had happened, the beast didn't show any sign of guilt, barely taking a moment to glance in my direction before dropping its head to the ground in an apparent search for food.

It occurred to me that I should attempt to locate my bag, in the hope it remained in one piece, and after the briefest of searches I found it, intact, lying on the track on the far side of the cart. However, my subsequent attempts at taking control of the horse in the hope I could ride it to safety were not so successful. Try as I might to approach it in a non-threatening manner, the beast repeatedly stepped back, away from me, with an insistent shake of the head. I would have tried dashing forward to take hold of the harness but my weakened condition and uncertain balance made that an impossibility and I suspected the horse knew it.

Since the repeated efforts at catching the animal had begun to make me feel weary, I decided not to expend any more energy on what appeared to be a hopeless task and gave thought to finding help on foot. As far as I could recall, we had not passed any buildings for some while prior to the accident, so it seemed the sensible thing to do was to continue forward, rather than double back. My mind made up, I hobbled off along the track, my headache no better and the cold, damp tendrils of the fog seeming to have reached into every part of my clothing.

*

I had been walking, if you can call it such, for thirty minutes, hopelessly lost and entirely disorientated, with my spirits as dampened as the weather, when I arrived at a fork in the road. My first thought was one of hope; hope that I would find a signpost and, thereby, a clear route to salvation. Even if it meant a further walk of some distance, I would at least have some certainty as to where I was heading. But a thorough search failed to reveal any such assistance and my hopes subsided once more.

Which way to go? I had nothing on which to base a decision and not even any notion as to how much difference it would in fact make. In an effort to garner some sort of basic information, I stumbled a little way down each leg of the fork, thinking perhaps I might find one of them tending to climb, as if it might be about to head up into the hills, which I considered not to be the best of options. But there was no discernable change in the incline in either case.

Still dithering, there came from the right-hand fork the sound of a sheep bleating. It was the first clear noise I had heard since the accident, so I took it as some sort of sign. Unscientific though it was, I continued my journey along the right fork. Of the sheep, there was subsequently no sign.

*

After another quarter of an hour, I found myself growing physically weak, a combination, I supposed, of my injuries and the relentless dampness in the air that had by now left my clothes sodden. I also found myself worrying more and more that I might suffer the effects of some hidden danger, perhaps stumbling over a sudden precipice and plunging to my death. It was, with hindsight, irrational, but the unnerving sense of danger grew upon me, little by little, until my nerves were in tatters. At one point I even stopped and sat on a section of stone wall so as to compose myself. For the first time on that hillside, alone, lost and beset by a growing sense of helplessness, I even began to wonder if I would make it back to civilisation alive. There were, after all, countless stories of lone walkers heading off on to a Scottish hillside, never to be seen or heard from again.

But as I began to contemplate the need for a second halt to pull myself together, a brief, though desperately welcome, gap opened up in the fog to my right. It was, in fact, more a series of small, irregular gaps, rather than one large one, but they were clustered close enough together to provide a reasonably clear view. And there, some way above me, was a house and one other building, quite likely a farm, I thought. It wasn't possible to make out a track that would take me up the side of the hill, but I felt all I needed to do now was keep a sharp eye out for any kind of track or path running away to my right.

My spirits soared and energy flooded back into my aching and tired body. After what seemed like an eternity wandering in the fog, I finally had hope of rescue and I recommenced my stumbling, urged on by real purpose, ignoring the pain in my head and the tiredness in my damp limbs.

And I didn't have far to go before I found a track leading off in generally the right direction through a break in the wall. It seemed moderately well used, shallow wheel ruts and hoof marks that looked fresh enough to be no more than a day old, which suggested there was a good chance of finding someone home. It seemed that at last my ordeal was over and I stepped on to the trackway filled with a sense of relief. But what happened between there and the farm buildings, I was not to know for some little while.

I had taken, perhaps, a dozen steps when the pain in my head became worse and my sense of balance began to fail me. The world started to veer wildly in all directions and my eyesight blurred to the point where I could make out nothing more than the general outline of trees and walls. The nausea in my nostrils and throat became intense and I realised I was falling into unconsciousness.

[illegible]

[illegible]

[illegible]

[illegible]

A FOREIGN DOCTOR

There was a time in my childhood when I fell out of a tree. It wasn't an especially big tree and I didn't fall a great way, but being only five years old at the time, the fall was far enough to do me harm. We had been playing hide and seek, had my younger sister and I, along with two of our cousins, who were staying with us during that summer week. I had dreamed up a plan that would, I thought, allow me to remain out of sight for the entire day, if I so desired. My thinking was that no one would ever guess to look up, into the trees. I was pleased to find that, for a while, it worked, but when trying to reach what I thought to be a better hiding place on a higher branch, I lost first my footing then my grip and plunged to the ground.

I can remember even now the sound of voices, but for some odd reason they didn't seem to be those of my sister and cousins. Instead, they seemed foreign, a peculiar language that I had never heard before, and there were many of them, chattering away in great excitement. They stopped without warning, before resuming much closer to me in low, careful tones, as if trying not to wake me.

On that occasion, the voices left me and I awoke to find

myself laid out on one of the sofa in our drawing room. Faces peered down at me, filled with concern, their lips moving but no sound reaching my ears. I soon drifted back into a state of unconsciousness, from which I awoke, I was subsequently told, over an hour later. My parents had been horrified by the whole affair and, said my sister with some relish, genuinely worried I might die. A bump on the head can, I learned later, be a very bad thing indeed.

Now it appeared the same scene was being played out all over again, different only in its particulars. Voices came to me in the darkness, swirling around me, snatches of words all that I could make out; never enough to make any sense. Then a great roar filled my head and I drifted back into the void.

It was the ticking of a clock that I heard next. Rhythmic and certain, it felt familiar and calming, easing me gently back into the world from which I had, until then, been absent. There were no voices this time, just the endlessly soothing ticking of the clock, calling me back from wherever it was I had been.

My eyes opened with a start, then shut just as quickly, as they were swamped with light so bright it made them hurt. My heart began to thump with alarm and it took me some moments to calm myself down. When I then felt up to the effort, I opened one eye just a little, allowing it time to adapt to the brightness, before I repeated the exercise with the other one.

There was, I observed, no more fog. Instead, I found myself looking up at a ceiling, white and uneven, where a small spider was busy spinning silk round what I took to be a fly. I watched it for a while, curious to see it work with such precision and speed. No doubt it had waited some time for its next victim to come along and now it had absolutely no intention of allowing it to escape from its clutches.

After a while, curiosity caused me to lower my gaze

and I found I was in a small, square room, sparsely furnished with a plain chest of drawers, a matching wardrobe and a single wicker chair that had seen better days. As for myself, I discovered that I was in a bed, my head propped up just a little on pillows that felt too soft for my liking. A collection of bed sheets and eiderdowns weighed down on my chest, almost pinning me in place. I managed, with a discomforting amount of effort, to wriggle myself partially free from their embrace.

I could only conclude, in the absence of any kind of confirmation, that I had collapsed on the track outside the farmhouse, where someone had discovered me and brought me inside. Of one thing I was sure: I was not in any of the bedrooms in my godparents' house. I wondered if word had been sent for them to come fetch me.

I was still contemplating my situation when a figure appeared in the open doorway. It was that of a man, so tall that he had to bend down a little to see fully into the room, and so wide as to fill most of the space where the door would otherwise have been. My eyes, still not yet fully accustomed to their new surroundings, struggled to make out any details of this new arrival and when I attempted to speak to him, nothing but a dry, hopeless croak could be heard, my mouth too parched to manage anything more. I coughed and when I looked back towards the doorway, the figure had gone.

My attempt to then sit up caused the pain in my head to flare up and I immediately eased myself back down in response. Perhaps it would be better to remain patient and wait for my rescuer to return. The spider, I noticed, had stopped spinning and was, instead, busy pulling the tidy bundle that was the encased fly up towards the little dent in the ceiling that I took for its lair.

*

Several minutes must have passed when the sound of footsteps on the stairs and of voices – two men, I thought – brought an end to my contemplation. I was keen to find out something about my hosts, to whom I owed my considerable thanks, and I looked towards the doorway with a growing sense of anticipation.

I was correct in identifying there were two men approaching the room, but the one who entered first was not the giant I had seen minutes before. He wasn't as tall, for one thing. He had black, curly hair, greying a little at the sides, and a large, thick moustache that didn't suit him. He was dressed much more smartly than the other man. As he entered the room, with the giant close behind, the thinner man paused, pushed his wire-framed glasses into place and spoke the first words I had heard since regaining consciousness.

"Ah, I see you are back in the land of the wakeful." I attempted to prop myself up again, the better to effect an introduction, but he wasn't happy for me to do so. "No, no. Please, you must not strain yourself. You need to rest. That is quite a blow you have taken to your head."

I put an end to my efforts to sit up, not without some sense of relief, and settled back on the soft pillows. As I did so, the smaller man picked up the lone chair in the room and put it next to the bed.

"You are no doubt wondering what on earth has happened and you most likely have a good many questions, so allow me to introduce myself. I am Dr Jens Sneijder and you are here in my home and surgery."

I reached out with my right hand, which the Doctor shook, his grip firm and confident.

"Alexander Templeman. I am very happy indeed to make your acquaintance, Doctor, though the circumstances are somewhat out of the ordinary." The words did not come easily, for my mouth remained dry.

My host turned towards the larger man, who passed him

a half-filled glass.

"Please, try drinking some water," said the Doctor, leaning across the bed and gently easing my head forward a little so that I could sip at the cool liquid. I'm not sure that a drop of water had ever been so welcome to me.

"The circumstances of our meeting are indeed somewhat unusual," continued the Doctor, placing the glass on the bedside cabinet. "My man here, Selkman, found you lying on the ground on the driveway. You were unconscious and covered in a good many cuts and bruises. Most peculiar. It was fortunate Selkman found you when he did. Much longer and the exposure may well have been your undoing."

I tilted my head towards the giant. "Thank you, Mr Selkman. It seems I owe a debt to you."

The giant remained impassive and silent.

"After examining you," continued Sneijder, "I diagnosed that you had received a concussion. There is a very large bump on the right side of your head, which you should take care not to bang again."

I raised my right hand to the area of my head referred to by the Doctor and dabbed with my fingertips at a large swelling that throbbed to the touch.

"No wonder I had such a terrible pain in my head," I observed, relieved at my good fortune to come upon a house occupied by a Doctor. After the misfortune that had brought me to the house, it made for a most welcome change in my luck.

"Do you recall how you acquired that bump, Mr Templeman?"

"Yes, I do. We were travelling in a farm cart when…" It was then that the full memory of what had happened came back to me with a start.

"Mr Templeman, are you alright?"

"Yes. Quite so. But there was another man," I blurted out.

"Another man?"

"Yes, the farm labourer driving the cart. There was an accident. The horse lost its nerve when something ran across the road and we crashed. I can't recall the details. But the labourer, Doctor. He's still there, lying in the road. How long have I been unconscious?"

My alarm concerned the Doctor, who held up a hand. "Careful, Mr Templeman. You must not excite yourself. It could cause complications. Now then, I would say you have been with us for a little over an hour. Of course, I cannot say how long you were lying on the drive. Where is this other man?"

I tried to piece together the journey I had made from the site of the accident to the farmhouse, but the truth was I could remember only fragments. Being lost as I was in the fog for so long, it left me feeling helpless.

"I don't know, Doctor. I know it sounds ridiculous, but it was the fog, you see. We made several stops for deliveries and we seemed to take such a convoluted route that I have no idea where we went or even where I am now. But it can't be far, I'm sure of that. My injuries, they stopped me from walking with any real speed."

I paused, recalling that I had tried and failed to find a pulse on the labourer.

"There is something more that you can now recall?" The Doctor spoke gently, seeming to know there was something terrible on my mind.

"There is. I tried to find a pulse on the man. I couldn't. And there was much blood on the road from a wound to his head."

"You fear the worst, I take it, Mr Templeman?"

"I do, I'm afraid."

"Well, let us see if we can't find this labourer."

Sneijder turned to face the giant and issued instructions for him to search the surrounding roads at once. I offered the only other piece of helpful information I could, informing them I had approached the house from the left as you left the drive. Without a word, Selkman went to carry out his mission.

"It can't be far," I repeated. "The fog, it was so heavy I could hardly see my feet."

"Indeed. The fogs here can be like those in Holland. So solid you could almost cut through them with a sharp knife. The fog has yet to lift and I fear it will not make Selkman's job an easy one, but he is a good man. I am sure he will find your friend."

The effort required to concentrate and converse began, even after so short a time, to cause me to feel tired. It must have shown on my face because Dr Sneijder stepped closer to the bed and held a hand against my forehead.

"We must be careful not to tax you too heavily, Mr Templeman." He retrieved the glass of water and brought it again to my lips. "Here, we need to ensure you consume sufficient fluids, otherwise your condition will only worsen."

I swallowed most of the water this time, eager to quench my thirst. The cool liquid felt good as it slipped down my throat and left me a little refreshed. The Doctor, however, was not to be persuaded to any other course of action than further rest for his unexpected patient.

"Now then, you must continue your rest," he went on, peering over the top of his glasses in the way only a Doctor or a teacher does. "Perhaps after a little more sleep we can think about helping you downstairs, so you can join me in the sitting room."

"But, I'm sure I can manage the stairs now," I began to say, only to find myself cut off at the pass.

"No, no, Mr Templeman. It is a common mistake to believe one has recovered from a concussion sooner than is, in fact, the case. It most often leads to complications; sometimes even death. You rest some more and when Selkman returns we can hear together his report."

I had barely dropped my head back on to the pillow and yet was already feeling drowsy. Perhaps the Doctor was right; I really wasn't anywhere near as well recovered as I had thought. As the Doctor picked up the empty glass and got to his feet, I closed my eyes and in what must have been mere seconds drifted off to sleep.

A SURPRISING REPORT

I awoke to the sound of someone chopping wood, or, at least, that was what I took it to be. A regular thumping and clefting as timber was split apart, coming from somewhere nearby but outside the part of the house I was quartered in. There was something deeply reassuring about it, in much the same way as listening to a ticking clock.

Feeling entirely refreshed and my headache almost completely gone, I sat up in bed and looked about me. There was a moment's relief as I found I was still in the bedroom I recollected from my last period of consciousness. After the morning's events, I would not have been altogether surprised to have awoken somewhere else entirely, once more with not the slightest idea how and when I had arrived there. Of one other thing I was also certain; I was famished.

As I pulled back the bed sheets and began to steady myself for an attempt at standing up, the bedroom door opened and I found myself once more facing Dr Sneijder. He stepped into the room and eyed me with interest, his hands in his pockets. He was, no doubt, sizing up his patient.

"And how do we feel now, Mr Templeman? A little better, I hope."

"Remarkably so, thank you, Doctor. The headache has almost entirely gone. The aches and pains also seem to have subsided. I owe you a debt, Doctor. You have obviously done a tremendous job."

"Ah, please, Mr Templeman, it was a straightforward diagnosis and the course of treatment clear to even the most junior of medical practitioners. I must admit, however, that I did help things along the way by giving you a sleeping draught a little earlier. There is always a temptation for patients suffering a concussion to believe they are recovered long before it is so and, as I mentioned earlier, that can lead to complications. I hope you will forgive me."

Sneijder sounded a little uncertain, there being some hesitation in his words. But he need not have worried on my account.

"Doctor, you will get no complaints from me. I'm aware I was in rather a bad way when your man found me and I'm only too grateful for your assistance and expertise. I thank my lucky stars that I should have been so fortunate as to stumble upon the home of a member of the medical profession."

My assurances seemed to do the trick and the awkwardness lifted from his shoulders at once.

"Well, that's very good to hear. Now then, you will, I suspect, be in need of a little food and perhaps a cup of that tea you English so enjoy. I must say, I am partial to it myself these days."

I could hardly have been happier when Sneijder mentioned food and drink. There was no need for him to present me with a vast array of the very best dishes; as far as I was concerned, anything edible would do very nicely indeed.

"I feel as if I could very well eat you out of house and

home, Doctor. I'm not a fussy eater. Anything you have to hand will do."

"Excellent. I will have a bowl of water, soap and some towels brought up to the room for you, so you can wash. Your clothes have been unpacked." He gestured towards the small walnut wardrobe up against the far wall. "If you would then like to join me downstairs, you can address your hunger and thirst and I can provide a report on what Selkman found on his searches."

Of course, the cart and the farm labourer. I wanted to know the news at once, but it seemed inappropriate to pursue the matter aggressively, so I held back and agreed to join the Doctor as soon as I was washed and dressed, which I then attended to with some haste.

*

Selkman was waiting for me in the hallway and, silent as ever, the brooding giant of a man led me down a set of wide, balustraded oak stairs, along a brightly-lit hall and into the sitting room, where my host was awaiting me, seated on a plain, high-backed chair that reminded me of one I used to climb over and under in my paternal grandparents' house as a small boy.

The room was large enough to accommodate comfortably perhaps a dozen people and was plainly decorated. It could be said to have lacked a feminine touch and struck me as being very functional. There was but one picture hanging on the walls, a large map of Europe, recently drawn I would say, and the volumes on a tall, narrow bookcase by the door were on practical subjects such as botany, archaeology and politics.

"Thank you, Selkman. You may leave us." The Doctor stood up and made his way to a small table adjacent to a window that looked out to the rear gardens. A tea service was set out for two. "How do you take your tea, Mr

Templeman?"

"With just a little milk, thank you Doctor. It's a very pleasant home you have here."

"It provides us with all that we need. I imagine it would be a little too old fashioned for some people, but I find it inoffensive, myself." He presented me with a cup of tea then collected the other for himself. "Please, take a seat. We have much to discuss."

It was strange, but now that I was more or less recovered, I seemed to see Sneijder afresh, noticing things about him that I had not before. He looked a little older than I initially thought, most likely beyond the age of fifty, as attested to by the prevalence of grey in his hair and moustache. His accent was more pronounced and, despite his excellent English, his words were not quite shaped correctly. But I could not very well complain about that since, aside from some very poor French, I spoke not a word of any foreign language. I also observed that his deportment was very correct, somewhat akin to that of a military man, which I put down to an undoubtedly strict schooling on the matter; I had a little experience of that myself.

Most of all, however, I was struck by the force of character that looked out at me through his penetrating brown eyes. It spoke of a man who was very certain of himself, as I supposed a good Doctor ought to be, and someone who, I thought likely, would not bear a fool at all lightly. It made me wonder quite what he really thought about me.

"Now then," proceeded Sneijder. "You will no doubt be wanting to hear what Selkman discovered on his search of the surrounding roads."

"I hope I was wrong in my judgement of the labourer's condition," I offered, thinking it might, in any case, have been too long a time since the accident occurred for someone with serious injuries to have survived in such harsh conditions.

"I am afraid we will not be able to confirm it either way, Mr Templeman."

I hesitated a moment, before replaying. "I'm not sure I understand you, Doctor."

"Unfortunately, Selkman was not able to locate the labourer or his horse and cart. He searched for some time, but, aside from the difficulty of the fog, the roads and trackways in these parts can be a considerable challenge to one's sense of direction. I wonder if perhaps you wandered, lost in the fog, for longer than you realised, Mr Templeman. If that were so, the scene of the accident could be a number of miles from here."

I was somewhat taken aback. I hadn't considered the possibility that I had been wandering, all but blind, in the fog for mile after mile. But, now the Doctor put the suggestion to me, it seemed entirely possible, especially as I had been suffering badly with a concussion and had little previous experience of the roads on which I had been travelling.

"I hadn't considered the possibility, Doctor, but, of course, I have no real idea how long I was lost or how far I travelled. I can't even say when it was that I collapsed on your driveway. I feel a little bad now about putting Selkman to such pains for what turned out to be no real purpose."

"No, no, Mr Templeman. It was quite the right thing to do. You should not reproach yourself. It is only unfortunate that Selkman was not able to locate the scene of the accident. But we should not despair. It is possible that some other traveller came upon the scene and called for assistance."

"I suppose you're right, Doctor. I know I am no medical man, but I am pretty certain the labourer had no pulse and there is no help to be given to a dead man, other than to arrange a proper funeral."

"Quite so. I hope you don't think me rude in asking, Mr Templeman, but where were you travelling to when the accident occurred? This is a somewhat isolated part of the country. Were you perhaps intent on enjoying a little walking and fishing?"

"I don't consider it rude at all, Doctor. You have every right to know a little about this stranger you have so generously taken in and restored to health."

I occupied the next several minutes explaining, no doubt in excessive detail, how I had arrived in a heap on the driveway to his house and where my intended destination was. The recounting of the tale helped to bring a little more order to my own mind of the events that had occurred since I left Pimlico only the day before.

"I am afraid to say that I am not familiar with your godparents' house, Mr Templeman, which makes me think again that you have probably travelled a greater distance than you initially believed. We are thirty minutes, at least, from New Cumnock. I will, of course, be happy to arrange for Selkman to take you back to the village in our horse and carriage once this fog has lifted enough to make travel a safe prospect and you are most welcome to remain our guest until then."

"Thank you, Doctor. That's very good of you. Do you think it will be long until this nuisance of a fog begins to lift?"

"I'm afraid to say they can sometimes be very persistent indeed. A day or two is entirely normal and, on one occasion last year, the same fog remained in place for five days, though there was the occasional teasing break. We have become quite used to them. I believe it is always better to work with nature than against it."

"Five days. That's remarkable. Let's hope it's nothing of the sort on this occasion."

"Indeed. Indeed." The Doctor sipped a little of his tea. "You didn't mention what work it is you do, Mr

Templeman, if you don't mind me asking."

"I'm training with a firm of solicitors in London. McMaster and Quarryman. Aim to have my own practice one day. Mind you, there are so many blessed exams to be passed, I could still be taking them in a decade's time."

"A solicitor." A smile appeared under that heavy moustache of his. "I shall try not to hold that against you."

"You'll be one of the few people not to. Seems we're not altogether a wholly appreciated bunch of people, unlike members of the medical profession. Doctor, your accent, it's been gnawing away at me, but try as I might, I just can't place it. Northern European, I would hazard a guess?"

"Ah, my apologies, Mr Templeman. Yes, I am from Holland. The town of Emmen, near the German border, to be a little more precise. Sad to say that most people have me marked down for a German whenever they guess where I am from."

"Ah, I've never yet paid a visit to Holland."

"A beautiful country, though it does, of course, rather lack the sort of hills one finds around here."

"That's true enough. Do I take it you practice here now, in Scotland?"

"I do indeed. This house is both my home and my surgery. I have been here in Scotland for a little over a year, which seems rather surprising now I come to think of it."

Since the Doctor seemed relaxed about discussing the matter, and as I was both curious and had little else to occupy me, I ventured to ask a few more questions. One presented itself to me almost immediately.

"You practice here? Surely you cannot have an awfully large number of patients in such a remote spot. Are your days terribly quiet?"

Sneijder laughed at the suggestion in a good-hearted manner before answering. "I am not in general practice, Mr

Templeman. I would, indeed, have very little business if that were the case. Not enough, I suspect, to pay the rental on this property. No, I specialise in treating patients with severe mental imbalances. Those for whom other more conventional treatments have proven to be ineffective. I developed my theories and practices in Holland and had been, for some little while, keen to try them elsewhere. A wealthy man from these islands approached me with an offer of employment. His wife was suffering with emotional difficulties that had failed to respond to numerous other treatments and a mutual friend suggested he might like to make an enquiry to me. It proved a most interesting case and gave me a means of establishing myself here."

"Ah, I see. And I suppose a quiet, out of the way spot like this is just the thing for a practice like yours?"

"Quite so. It is essential that my patients have as few distractions as possible and access to plenty of fresh air and outdoor activities such as walking. The Scottish Highlands seemed a little too remote, but this part of the country is ideal, while this house has sufficient bedrooms and other rooms to accommodate both my household and my patients."

"Do you have patients here now? I don't recall seeing anyone else apart from you and Selkman."

"There are indeed, though you will understand I cannot share any particulars with you. It is rather likely that you will meet one or two, but I will leave it up to them to decide whether or not they wish to share their names."

"Of course, I entirely understand. Your patients' privacy must be respected."

"Apart from myself and Selkman there is also a housekeeper, Mrs Rafferty. You will meet her shortly as she is preparing a meal for you as we speak."

"Well, I don't want to get in your way, Doctor. If it helps, I would be entirely amenable with the suggestion I remain in my room for the greater part of my time here, while we wait for this fog to lift. I certainly wouldn't want to cause your patients any inconvenience. I can imagine it might come as an unwelcome surprise to some of them to find me here."

"That will not be necessary, Mr Templeman. Patients are free to come and go as they please when they are not undergoing treatment, so it is entirely up to each of them to decide whether or not they wish to meet you. I will, of course, ensure they know of your presence here."

There came a shuffling sound from behind me, one that caught the Doctor's attention.

"Ah, Mrs Rafferty, there you are with Mr Templeman's luncheon. I hope it is agreeable to you, Mr Templeman. Some cheese and bread, with a few fruits. It is not long until dinner, so we did not want to push a large meal on to you now."

"It will do very nicely indeed, thank you. I feel now as if I could eat several meals, one straight after the other, I'm so hungry."

The housekeeper made space for the plate and cutlery on the small table where the tea service was already positioned. She was a surly-looking woman. I had no wish to be uncharitable, but I had the immediate impression that I would not care to cross swords with her. Though not tall, she was distinctly stocky, with hands that were heavily worn, no doubt by years of labour. I considered that she was most likely in her late forties or perhaps early fifties. Her hair was a mass of unkempt mousey-brown, which she kept in some sort of order by enclosing it in a floral headscarf that had seen better days. I got the impression, from the way the woman looked at me, that she considered me an unwelcome, albeit temporary, addition to the household. It occurred to me that my arrival might have undermined her, no doubt carefully made, plans for the provisioning of the house.

"Well, I must press on with my work," said Sneijder, getting to his feet. "I have an appointment with one of my patients shortly and there is much to be done in preparation. Please feel free to avail yourself of our, admittedly rather limited, facilities, Mr Templeman. There are some books there in the bookcase and there will be a newspaper somewhere here. Dinner will be at six-thirty and, if you would like to join us here, I will introduce you to any of the patients who feel up to meeting you."

"I look forward to it and I really can't thank you enough, Doctor. You've been a most hospitable host."

As the Doctor and his housekeeper left the room together, I turned to my meal and tucked in with relish. Breakfast seemed by then to have been such a very long time ago.

A GUEST FOR DINNER

I arrived in the sitting room a little before six-thirty. Although I had no recollection of doing so, I had managed to keep hold of my suitcase as I stumbled around the countryside in the fog, following the accident. One welcome advantage of this was that I was able to change into some clean and more suitable clothes for dinner.

My spirits took a distinct upward lift at the sight of a man and a woman occupying two of the chairs in the room. Although I would have hesitated to admit it to any of the Doctor's patients, I was, in fact, a little keen to meet one or two of them; based, I must add, on nothing other than a curious interest in the treatments Sneijder was providing in such an isolated location. Since I had a passing interest in the works of Sigmund Freud, I found the opportunity to speak to patients in the process of undergoing such a regime distinctly appealing. I was somewhat embarrassed to find myself immediately contemplating how I might go about eliciting information from them as to their treatment, without appearing to be rude and intrusive.

"Ah, Mr Templeman, you are in good time," Doctor Sneijder spoke as he arrived at my shoulder. I hadn't noticed he'd entered the room and his appearance caused me to flinch. "Excellent. In that case, allow me to introduce you to two of our current guests."

The other two people in the room, who had now noticed the arrival of myself and Sneijder, got to their feet and turned to face us.

"This is Mr Harold Duncan. He has been with us for a week now. And allow me to introduce Mrs Camilla Downing. Mrs Downing is very nearly at the end of her treatment and we entertain high hopes she will be leaving us within the next two or three days. Mr Duncan and Mrs Downing, please meet Mr Alexander Templeman, our most recent and somewhat unexpected arrival, though a very welcome guest, all the same."

I had feared being as welcome as a bachelor at a dinner party, where all the other guests are married couples, but neither of my two new acquaintances showed any sign of hostility, which put my mind at ease on that score.

The Doctor led us without delay through to the dining room, which was large enough to accommodate a dozen guests, or so I judged. It was just the four of us for dinner, which was a simple affair, beginning with French onion soup, followed by lamb cutlets, then a dessert of sherry trifle, which, from the look of total satisfaction that appeared on his face, Sneijder enjoyed most of all.

Although I am not the greatest of conversationalists, I am usually a willing participant during a meal, since it would be rude to be anything else. However, conversation on this occasion was rather sparse and sporadic and I did wonder at times if my presence was the cause of this, especially as my less than subtle attempts to find out a little something about the nature of Harold Duncan's and Camilla Downing's medical problems and their treatment elicited exceedingly brief answers that gave away nothing at all. Out of a sense of guilt and embarrassment, I attempted to steer the conversation on to, first, the quality of the shooting and fishing in the area and then, out of near desperation, revisiting my recent adventures. Neither subject piqued the interest of the two patients, although the Doctor was good enough to humour me and asked a question or two.

With dinner finished, we returned to the sitting room to take coffee and spirits, of which there seemed to be a plentiful supply; indeed, the breadth of the offering was most impressive for such an isolated house. It was while the housekeeper brought through our coffee and Sneijder attended to the spirits that I took the opportunity to assess my two reticent dinner guests afresh, perplexed as I was at their odd state of mind during the meal.

Harold Duncan was a man I judged to be in his early forties, going by the thinning nature of his short, brown hair and the lines that were starting to make their presence known on his forehead. He was a remarkably slender man; indeed, so much so that, given his greater than average height, I feared he might snap in half during a high wind. Whenever I tried to engage him in conversation, he would look at me through his wire-framed glasses, his wide, weepy eyes seemingly unable to focus properly, and answer, mostly with a single short sentence and never with more than two.

I did manage to ascertain that he was from Dorking in Surrey and worked for one of the country's leading newspapers, but more was not forthcoming, despite several attempts on my part to dig a little deeper. There was a flicker of something more in his eyes, perhaps a sign of real contentment, when Sneijder asked him how he liked the trifle and when I mentioned that I enjoyed the occasional game of cricket, he managed a thin, if briefly lived, smile as he mentioned that he had watched a day's play during an England test match against Australia in 1909.

But, on the whole, I felt I knew nothing more about the

newspaper man as we sat there in the living room than I had upon first meeting him. I didn't like to suppose that he was seeking to deliberately keep things from me, but it is not altogether a normal experience to learn so little about a person during the course of an evening when there are only four of you in the room. Indeed, it wasn't even as if he had dominated the conversation with his own questions, since he had asked very few about me.

As I sat there watching him, he began to stir two cubes of sugar into his coffee, an excessively long, drawn out process that suggested he was afraid a single grain might remain intact when he came to drink the coffee. It was the kind of obsessive behaviour that I witnessed in a chap I used to know at the office, who would become uncommonly agitated when something was not entirely right. A sheaf of papers that were not precisely in alignment or a speck of dust on the toe of a shoe. There had been a day the previous September when he stopped coming into the office and we were later informed he had experienced a nervous breakdown. We never saw nor heard from him again. A sad case, indeed.

Having taken a minute or two to cast an eye over Duncan, I then turned my attention to the very different figure of Camilla Downing. A short and somewhat plump woman whom I judged to be in her mid-thirties, she had rather lovely auburn hair that she kept piled high with an assortment of pins, rather in the style of the day.

If Duncan had been a challenge to engage in conversation, he was, by comparison with Downing, something of a chatterbox. I found the woman almost impossible to extract a word from. I deployed all my very best efforts, even attempting to converse on matters of speculative gossip I had noticed in the newspapers in recent weeks and the latest ladies' fashions, but she never took the bait and would slip away, to drift once more deeper waters, where she lurked silent and beyond my reach.

In matter of fact, it was Sneijder who told me most about her. Her husband had arranged for Mrs Downing to visit Sneijder's premises after her debilitating emotional and mental problems had defeated the best efforts of other doctors, some of them well known in their field. It seemed Mr Downing occupied a senior post as a civil servant in the War Office and was somewhat concerned that his wife's disturbing condition might limit his progress into more senior posts. Of course, added Sneijder, Mr Downing had not put things quite like that himself, but it had been clear to even the most casual of observers what his motives were.

But what I found most odd, you could even say disturbing, about Mrs Downing was the entirely vacant look in her eyes. It was as if they were no more than a facade, beyond which there lay an empty structure. Her movements too were strange; somewhat slow and laborious, as if she was having to engage in an abnormal amount of effort in order to exert proper control over her limbs.

All in all, things struck me as being very odd and I had a thought that I was rather grateful I didn't need to avail myself of the specialist services of Dr Sneijder, since it seemed to entail the complete breaking down of a person's character, leaving them something of a hollowed-out husk. I could only hope he rebuilt each individual before they left his care. Lord knows what their families and friends would think if they arrived home in the state Duncan and Downing were in that evening.

We idled away another twenty minutes or so over coffee and further stilted conversation, before Sneijder stood up and announced that it was time for his two patients to be retiring for the night.

"It is most important, Mr Templeman, that all my patients get a full night's sleep. There must be no exceptions, not even when we have the excitement of an unexpected guest. Otherwise, it can undermine all the hard work both I and my patients put into their recovery."

I exchanged good evenings with the two patients and looked on as Sneijder ushered them out of the room, speaking in such a low voice that I could not make out a single word. Not that I had any need to hear what was said, of course.

"Well, now then, Mr Templeman, will you stay on for a while and join me in another glass or two? It would make a pleasant change to be able to spend some time conversing with someone other than my patients. Or, for that matter, Selkman and my housekeeper; neither of whom are the greatest of conversationalists. If I am to be honest, it can get a little dull at times," he added, his voice lowered, while he looked towards the doorway in an exaggerated manner.

"My pleasure, Doctor. I feel as if I have slept for England already today and I would be only too happy to see if I'm up to the challenge of matching your wits sufficiently so as not to bore you."

"Excellent. Another coffee, or can I tempt you with a whiskey?"

"I don't mind if I try a drop of your whiskey, thank you very much."

While Sneijder attended to our drinks, I noticed again the map hanging on the wall. It prompted a question I felt a sudden urge to have answered.

"I've never had the pleasure of visiting Holland, Doctor, but, tell me, is it really as flat as they say it is? No hills at all?"

For a moment, Sneijder's shoulders shook a little, then he turned towards me, a glass in each hand, and replied with a good deal of humour in his voice. "Yes, Mr Templeman, I can assure you it really is a very flat country indeed. I am sure there is a very small incline here and there, but they are few and far between and rarely encountered." He handed me my drink and we saluted the fog.

"I suppose the closest we have here to match that is East Anglia. Once you get beyond Peterborough it is as flat as a table-top all the way to the sea. I'm not sure there's anywhere else in the country that's quite like it."

"Ah, yes. I have heard of East Anglia, of course, but I have not yet had the pleasure of visiting that part of the country. It sounds positively ideal, should I happen to ever feel homesick."

The Doctor sat down in the chair opposite me, loosened his tie with some relish, then breathed in the peaty scent of the whiskey. "Such a wonderful aroma," he observed, with real feeling. "You can, as they say, smell the peat upon which much of this part of the country is built."

"My godfather would certainly agree with you there. He's a whiskey man through-and-through."

We each took a moment to savour our drinks, the warmth of the alcohol playing across my tongue before igniting in my throat. There was not a better drink for a time when the weather pressed in, chill and wet.

"Tell me, Templeman, if you don't mind, what do you think about all this talk of war? Do you think it will really come to that?"

War? It was, indeed, a subject of regular discussion in the newspapers and increasingly so at dinner parties and the like, but I tried not to think about it too much. For one thing, given my age, I was bound to be expected to volunteer if it came to that and, whilst I would naturally not hesitate to do so, I was no budding hero. The thought of being blown to pieces on some faraway battlefield did not much appeal to me. I was rather anticipating a long and happy life.

"I should hope not, Doctor. It seems to me it's rather difficult to see how it would be in anyone's best interests."

"But the situation in the Balkans looks most delicate. Some suggest it will only take the smallest of provocations to ignite things and up it will all go, like a powder keg. You have hopes, then, it can be resolved peacefully?"

"All that is needed, surely, is for all concerned to remain calm and talk things through in a level-headed manner. I would imagine it will probably help to keep the professional soldiers and sailors out of the room too. I think sometimes they get rather bored cooped up in their barracks and on their ships with no wars to fight."

"A war brought on by boredom, then? An interesting theory, indeed," he guffawed, such a show of emotion catching me off guard for a moment.

"It wouldn't surprise me if that very thing hasn't happened many times before," I added, in mock indignation, glad to see that the evening was livening up somewhat.

"That's not a line of thought I believe I have read in the newspapers, though now you suggest it I think they ought to consider it."

I returned for a moment to my whiskey, before adding, in a more serious tone, "I can't see the Kaiser being stupid enough to take on the might of the British Empire, can you? Germany may be a revitalised power since unification, but it is still no match for us."

"I am not so sure. On the continent there is a good deal of nervousness about the situation and a sense that some people are anxious indeed to go to war as soon as the opportunity presents itself."

The Doctor fingered one end of his moustache, his eyes downcast, and for a moment he seemed deep in thought.

"Am I to understand thoughts of war are altogether nearer the surface on the continent than they are here, Doctor?"

"I am afraid they are, yes indeed. Very many people live in full expectation there will be a war before the year is out and there are so many intertwined treaties that as soon as any two parties commit, it will be sure to bring in many, many more."

The Doctor sounded now somewhat despondent, the ease and humour of a moment ago now gone from his voice.

"Well, let's hope that people in high places who can take the necessary action to avoid a war breaking out do just that. It can't be beyond the wit of the best brains available to each party to sort out some sort of agreement that is to everyone's satisfaction."

"Yes, quite so. Let's hope you're right about that."

The conversation moved on to other subjects after a while and the Doctor's happy demeanour returned, especially when we alighted on the subject of politicians and, in particular, how the services of someone such as himself could be put to good use in flushing out of their heads all the many mad schemes they seemed forever able to dream up.

Eventually, as the clock on the mantelpiece chimed to let us know it was ten o'clock, the Doctor rose to his feet, a little unsteady, if I say so, and bade me goodnight. Breakfast, he informed me, was at eight sharp. Although I did not notice it at the time, by now all my earlier thoughts of how odd Duncan and Downing had appeared had left me entirely and I retired to my bed as relaxed and content as a man could be.

A BEAUTIFUL PATIENT

As I drew back the curtains on the following morning, fully refreshed after a splendid night's sleep, I did so in full expectation that a clear, bright dawn would greet me through the window. I was to be entirely disappointed, for the fog seemed anchored to the spot, entirely unwilling to shift so much as an inch. I could not even, in all honesty, propose that the situation had improved in any manner whatsoever, for the fog blotted out the view just as effectively as it had the day before.

My heart sank and shoulders slumped. Was the blessed thing never going to clear? A day's stay with Doctor Sneijder and his patients was an entertainment, but I was already beginning to feel that a second day would be both an imposition on the Doctor and, frankly, a bore to myself. I longed to be with my godparents, who were, no doubt, wondering where on Earth I was. A deep sigh escaped my lips and the energy with which I had arisen began to ebb away. I supposed that I had at least breakfast to look forward to. Small mercies and all that.

I made my way down the stairs and along the hallway in a somewhat dejected mood but, as soon as I entered the dining room, my spirits lifted. There, already sitting at the table, was a picture of pure beauty; a young woman so delightful to behold that I would have been heartless in the extreme not to have felt revitalised. Blonde hair, pinned in place so as to keep the neck exposed in the fashion of the day, framed a beautiful face blessed with a small, slender nose and classically high cheek bones. And as for the woman's eyes, they were, rather ironically, as blue as the sky on the clearest of days.

However, as has always been the way for me, no sooner had I delighted in such an uplifting sight than I began to feel distinctly awkward, for I am easily intimidated by such beauty. I ran a thumb along the inside of the opposite lapel on my jacket, set a welcoming smile on my face that I hoped did not make me look ridiculous and stepped forward to take a seat at the table, opposite my lone breakfast companion.

"Good morning," I offered in a casual tone that I hoped belied my discomfort. "My I join you?"

"A very good morning to you, sir. Of course. Please don't stand on ceremony on my behalf."

She spoke with a soft voice that hinted at a degree of hesitation, which at once had me remembering my ineffectual conversations of the previous evening.

"Alexander Templeman," I said, by way of introduction.

"Delighted to meet you, Mr Templeman. I am Miss Elizabeth Fitzsimon. I've already heard something about you from Dr Sneijder."

"Oh, dear. I hope it didn't make me look too hopeless a case. Falling out of a cart and getting lost in the fog doesn't present me in the most positive light."

A little laugh escaped her lips before she could stop it, which caused her cheeks to colour with a modest flush of red.

"I'm sorry, Mr Templeman, I'm sure it must have been

quite an experience and not at all funny."

"I don't suppose I was the greatest hero there's ever been. But I seem to have finished up in the ideal situation here, with a Doctor to patch me up."

"Indeed."

It was a single word, spoken in an odd and unexpected manner. Miss Fitzsimon then went quiet and returned to her scrambled eggs and bacon. I was going to ask her if I had said something wrong, but at that point the housekeeper arrived with more breakfast provisions, which she set out on the table, before giving me a sharp look through those dark, piercing eyes of hers. As soon as she had left the room, I set about loading food on to my plate and pouring myself a cup of coffee, the deep, strong aroma of which was excellent.

"Are you another of the Doctor's patients?" I enquired of Miss Fitzsimon. "That is, if you don't mind me asking."

She looked at me over the top of her tea cup and hesitated. To say I was perplexed by the sudden about turn in her manner would be putting things rather mildly, after we had got off to such a fine start. I wondered what on earth I had said that could have caused such a reaction.

"I am. Though I think my father worries too much about me." There was another pause. "He thinks I am unbalanced."

"Ah, fathers are, I think, often extremely concerned about the health of their daughters," I replied at once, keen to pick up our conversation. "My own father has always kept an eagle eye on my sister, whereas I could fall out of the tallest tree or down the longest flight of stairs and all he would do would be to tell me to get up and dust myself off."

"My father is used to getting things his own way. He is Sir Eustace Fitzsimon, the industrialist. You may have heard of him."

"Fitzsimon, you say." I thought on things for a moment

before the penny dropped. "Of course. My word, he's a very wealthy man. Must own quite a few of the many thousands of factories scattered across this great island of ours."

"He does, indeed. However, he only has two daughters and no son, something about which he often feels sad."

"Well, he should consider himself a lucky man to have two daughters rather than none at all. I'm sure my sister would agree with me on that score."

"I saw Selkman carrying you into the house."

"Me? You mean yesterday morning?"

"That's right. You looked to be in a very bad way. I even thought… well, you know, I thought for a moment the worst might have happened."

"You have the advantage of me there. I don't remember a thing of it. The last I can remember is struggling up the first part of the driveway, very unsteady on my feet, then I suppose I must have collapsed. The next thing I was aware of was waking up in one of the bedrooms."

"I hope you don't think I'm being rude, but I would be very keen to hear from you what happened. Doctor Sneijder was rather sparse on the detail when he spoke to me last night."

I gave Miss Fitzsimon an abbreviated account of my adventures, which she appeared to find most exciting, a reaction which, I must admit, I found quite appealing. I was all too aware that I could hardly claim to be the world's greatest adventurer. Missing the last bus home and having to walk along streets in London that I would normally choose to avoid at a late hour had, until then, been about as great an adventure as I had ever experienced; certainly in adult life.

The unknown whereabouts of the labourer who I had left lying in the road clearly held a particular interest for Miss Fitzsimon, who wasted no time in speculating as to the possibilities, displaying a lively mind in the process. As for myself, further recollection of the event caused me once more to feel somewhat guilty, especially as Selkman had not been able to locate the poor man.

Our conversation was, nonetheless, proceeding very pleasantly and my sense of awkwardness had all but dissipated when Doctor Sneijder arrived in the room and joined us at the table. He had, it transpired, already eaten, but was happy to take a cup of coffee while he sat with us. Sadly, his arrival seemed to put Miss Fitzsimon back into her shell and she added little more to the conversation before, shortly after the Doctor's appearance, she bade me a good morning and left for her room.

"Miss Fitzsimon arrived with us only two days ago," observed the Doctor, once she had left the room. "A charming young lady and one I am sure we can help."

"She mentioned she is the daughter of the industrialist Sir Eustace Fitzsimon."

"That is true. I was recommended to Sir Eustace by a friend of his, who had seen a family member benefit greatly from their treatment here. It is deeply rewarding to find such personal recommendations being made. It gives you encouragement that the methods one has spent so long developing and improving are bringing relief and happiness to a good many people."

There must at that point have been something of the Devil about me, because I could not resist the temptation to prod a little at the Doctor's confidence in his methods and, indeed, the need for them in all the cases sent to him.

"Miss Fitzsimon seems to be a little surprised that her father should feel she needs the attentions of a Doctor such as yourself. She did seem to me rather… normal just now."

I marshalled the last of my kippers on to the fork and waited for a reply, which came after only the briefest of pauses.

"It is common for a patient to believe they have nothing whatsoever wrong with them, especially, I might add, where female patients are concerned." There was just a hint of irritation in the Doctor's voice, but I avoided the natural temptation to look up and meet his stare, concentrating, instead, on despatching the final remnants of my breakfast. "Rarely does a patient experiencing emotional and mental stress and unease have any appreciation themselves of what ails them. Indeed, they often believe they are as normal and ordinary as you or I, Mr Templeman. Fortunately, in most cases my own methods allow me to bring a patient to some sort of understanding and awareness of their illness, which, in turn, helps them to manage it once they have left here.

"You are not able then to completely cure them? Surely that risks a relapse?"

It hadn't occurred to me up until then that patients would leave Sneijder's care without first being entirely cured, though why I should have expected otherwise was irrational, of course. There are a good many illnesses doctors cannot cure entirely or, in some unfortunate cases, cure at all.

"I am pleased to say that it has been a long time since a patient left me without first making considerable progress, but I am not able to effect miracles. I am sure you understand. Most patients make a full recovery and have no need of mine or any other Doctor's services to further treat their condition, but some, though they make excellent progress, continue to face challenges and it is then my duty to ensure they are equipped with the means to manage their condition effectively."

"I didn't mean to give offence, Doctor. Your speciality is something about which I know next to nothing and I'm afraid I may, as a result, sometimes ask silly questions."

"No offence taken, Mr Templeman. It is, indeed, a most complex matter, the human mind; one that I expect we will still be struggling to understand fully in a hundred years' time."

He glanced at his pocket watch, then placed his cup back on the saucer with great care. "Well, I really must leave you to yourself, Mr Templeman. I have my first appointment of the morning to prepare for. You will, of course, have noticed the fog remains with us." We both looked towards the nearest window, through which only the merest hint of garden greenery could be seen.

"I'm afraid it looks, for the time being," continued Sneijder. "as though you will be spending a second day with us. You should feel free to come and go as you wish. All I ask is that you cause no unease to the patients. They can be absent-minded and difficult to converse with once they are more than a few days into their treatment. Some people find it a little disconcerting."

"Rest assured, Doctor I have no wish to disturb your practice or in any way cause any of the patients unease. I'm very appreciative of your assistance and will be only too happy to recommence my journey once this blessed fog begins to lift."

"Well, let's both pray then for a strong wind to blow in off the sea, or else I may have to insist on you joining me in a hand of cards after dinner this evening."

With the Doctor gone, I mused over my encounter with Elizabeth Fitzsimon, a woman who seemed to me to be entirely without emotional or mental incapacity. Had her father sent her to Sneijder in the hope of dampening permanently the high spirits of a young daughter he perhaps found a concern? Or had I, as the Doctor suggested, altogether missed something in Miss Fitzsimon's character?

As I emptied my cup of the little coffee that remained, I observed, at the far end of the long hallway, Dr Sneijder open the door to what I took to be his surgery and then, holding her by the hand, lead Mrs Downing, who looked to be in some sort of trance, into the room. Unhappily, before I could begin to consider what I had just seen, the housekeeper arrived in the room once more and seemed to have realised where my gaze was cast, for she gave me such a look of disapproval that I felt distinctly uneasy. I placed my cup in its saucer and returned to my room without delay.

SUSPICIONS AROUSED

Having reviewed my limited supply of clothes and other items, I gave serious consideration to making an attempt at finding my own way back to New Cumnock. In my favour, I was by this time fully recovered from my experiences of the previous day, my headache having long since cleared up and the various knocks and bruises I suffered being only minor in nature. I also considered that even if the journey entailed covering as many as ten miles, it was hardly a route march and I was, as previously mentioned, carrying only the smallest of suitcases.

Against me was my very limited knowledge of the surrounding area, an apparent lack of any signposts that might help me and an awareness that my journey from the railway station had been a somewhat convoluted one. Of most concern, however, was the continuing fog, the denseness of which had not abated one bit since my arrival at the Doctor's residence.

On balance, I decided, a solo attempt would be foolhardy and almost certainly doomed to failure. At worst, I could become entirely lost on the hillsides, there to perish from exposure. I wasn't brave enough to take such a risk, especially when it was not absolutely necessary, so I decided, with some reluctance, to stay put.

Within an hour of returning to my room, I had grown bored of the book I'd taken with me from the sitting room, as well as my contemplating possible means of finding my way to my godparents' house. I was quite at a loose end and becoming restless, so I made my way back down the stairs and tried a turn around the gardens. But that was not a pleasant experience in the chill and damp of the fog. I followed that up by making my way back inside the house, to the sitting room, where I had a stab at the crossword in the previous day's newspaper. Unfortunately, I have never been one for such cryptic challenges and, in some degree of frustration, slapped the newspaper down on to the coffee table, jumped to my feet and began, for the umpteenth time, to peruse the books in the Doctor's small collection.

"They are not exactly thrilling, are they?"

The voice was that of a man and not one I'd heard before. I swung around and found myself looking into the puffy face of a bulbous, almost entirely bald man whom I judged to be in his late fifties. He was looking closely at me, as if his eyesight was very poor, and standing a little too close for comfort. I would have taken half a step back, but the bookcase blocked my retreat.

"James Scurry," he announced, in a stiff, formal voice as he thrust his right hand out towards me.

"Alexander Templeman," I replied. His grip was overly firm and I was glad when he released it.

"Ah, you're the chap, are you? Doctor Sneijder mentioned you were somewhere on the premises. Surprised I'd not met you sooner. I hear you had a bit of an accident on the road somewhere hereabouts." He spoke with a distinct though soft Scottish accent that had me wondering if he might be part of Sneijder's staff.

"I did, indeed. The fog spooked our horse and the driver lost control. I made it as far as this house purely by chance and collapsed at the end of the driveway. It seems I couldn't have stumbled upon a better place, what with it being the premises of a Doctor."

"You certainly did that. Fortune smiles on the brave, or so they say. Take a seat, Mr Templeman, so I can interrogate you properly." He produced a handkerchief from a pocket and blew his large, fat nose. It was to be something he did with exceeding frequency.

As we sat down, I sought to clarify his status in the household. "Are you part of Doctor Sneijder's staff?"

He laughed and shook his head. "Ah, that would be a fine thing, but I don't suppose the Doctor would be too happy about that, what with me being a patient and all that. I've been here three days now. Quite a pleasant little spot. I've stayed in worse places, that's for sure."

It was a wonder that, following three days of treatment, he still seemed inclined to engage in proper conversation with me, given my prior experience with Sneijder's patients. My boredom and frustrations began to lift a little.

"How have you been getting along with the Doctor's methods? They seem to be a little unusual, from what I can gather."

"Quite so. They are certainly new to me. But he comes with a high recommendation. I'm personal secretary to Lord Egremont and it was he who sent me here after I collapsed one afternoon last month. I told his lordship it was just indigestion, but he insisted he'd seen the symptoms before. Overwork and stress, he said. Then, when he heard about Doctor Sneijder, he insisted on paying for me to receive treatment here. A very generous man, wouldn't you say?"

Lord Egremont was a name I'd seen often in the newspapers, since he owned the Blue Kite Shipping Line, a considerable enterprise with routes between the mother country and most of our largest overseas territories. My parents had travelled on one of his liners several years ago.

"Yes, I'd say that is most generous. I don't know what Doctor Sneijder charges by way of fees, but I should imagine they are considerably more than I could afford, should the need ever arise."

"Will you be staying with us long? Only, I don't get much in the way of conversation out of that Duncan fellow and the ladies aren't interested in sports and politics."

"I would like to be on my way right now," I replied, glancing again out of the window, "but the damned fog just won't let up. I've never seen anything like it."

"Ah, it's always worst here on the west coast. In Edinburgh, the fogs are nowhere near so frequent, though they can sometimes be pretty thick. But I thought the fogs in London were the worst of all. Is that not so?"

"They can be pretty bad, to be fair, but I've not yet experienced one as bad as this."

"You'd better look out, or the Doctor will have you in his room at the end of the corridor there, swinging his watch in front of your face, and before you know it you'll be under his spell."

Scurry laughed, his eyes almost disappearing in the folds of his face as his cheeks rose to meet his drooping eyelids. A swinging watch, was it? So hypnosis was part of Sneijder's treatment. I wanted to know more, but before I could follow up with a question, Scurry noticed the newspaper I'd dropped.

"Good God, are they talking again about the Balkans and war? We should leave them to it, I say. Let them come to blows, if that's what they want to do, and keep the British Empire well out of things. Lord Salisbury got it right with Splendid Isolation, is what I say. How about you, Templeman? Think we should keep our noses out of things that don't concern us?"

He looked at me in much the same way as he had done by the bookcase, his eyes all but daring me to disagree.

"I think the best possible outcome would be for no one

to go to war," I proposed. "I'm sure we could offer to mediate. Let sense prevail."

I would have preferred not to have engaged in talk of war, for it was hardly an uplifting subject. Death and destruction never is. I had lost an uncle in the fighting in South Africa during the 1890s and had no desire to see any more of my relatives succumb to death or injury in further armed conflict. However, I could not deny it was often the subject of conversation at social gatherings and it occupied more than its fair share of space in the newspapers.

Scurry and I would, no doubt, have continued our conversation had not Sneijder appeared in the doorway to remind his patient that he had a consultation booked for ten-fifteen and it was, by then, ten-eighteen. Scurry made his apologies for having to bring our first meeting to an end and expressed a whole-hearted desire to pick up the thread of our conversation just as soon as the Doctor had finished with him. He then followed Sneijder along the corridor and disappeared into the room at its end.

*

I remained in the sitting room, composing a letter to Caroline, so that I would have something to send to her just as soon as I was able to reach a post office. I was certain she would be anxious to hear from me and was no doubt already wondering why I had not sent word of my safe arrival with my godparents. I wasn't at all keen on causing her alarm by explaining the precise cause of my delay, beyond the fog, which made it something of a challenge to justify my tardiness in sending her word of my arrival.

As I began to close the letter, the door to Sneijder's surgery opened and Scurry reappeared, listening intently to something the Doctor was saying to him, before turning and heading back towards the sitting room. I folded the letter in two and slipped it into a pocket in my jacket, before standing ready to welcome back my new acquaintance.

As far as transformations go, Scurry's was quite astonishing. He seemed nothing like the man I had been speaking to not much more than half an hour earlier. The free conversation was gone, replaced by the same short utterances I had received from Camilla Downing and Harold Duncan over dinner. Scurry too had that same vacant look in his eyes and seemed unable now to hold eye contact with me. I was taken aback at the change and that same sense of unease I experienced over dinner returned to worry away at me again.

After not more than ten minutes seated in the same armchair as before, Scurry closed his eyes and drifted off to sleep, snoring quietly as he did so. I yawned and stretched my arms out in front of me. Perhaps he had the right idea. A short nap would while away half an hour or so. As I considered the possibility, Sneijder stepped out of his office, disappeared into one of the other rooms, then emerged with the housekeeper; the two of them proceeding to make their way upstairs.

I stared at the closed door to Sneijder's surgery, all at once engulfed by a strong desire, no, a compelling need, to see beyond it. I checked that Scurry was still asleep before climbing quietly to my feet and making my way stealthily along the hallway, casting a furtive glance up the stairs as I arrived outside the surgery door. There was no sign of either Sneijder or the housekeeper. My hand was warmed and moistened by a thin film of sweat as I took hold of the door handle and tested it to see if it was locked. The handle turned without resistance and I felt the click of the bolt as it slid back from the frame.

I hesitated, conscious that I was about to intrude on the Doctor's privacy, which seemed a poor way to repay the man for the assistance he had so freely given me. Indeed, if it had been simple curiosity alone that pushed me forward then I hope I would have come to my senses and left things well alone. But it wasn't mere curiosity that had taken me to that door. The peculiar behaviour of Sneijder's patients had left me feeling perplexed, even a little concerned, but the remarkable alteration I had just witnessed in Scurry, I found deeply disturbing. And on top of all that, there was the odd way in which Elizabeth Fitzsimon had responded during our conversation over breakfast, when I mentioned how fortunate I was to have found myself in the good Doctor's hands after my misfortunes.

Perhaps my concerns were exaggerated, but I felt as if what lay beyond that door would settle the matter for me, one way or the other. Another glance up the stairs, also straining my ears in an effort to pick out any sounds that might hint at either the Doctor's or the housekeeper's imminent return, then I pushed the door open and, without any further hesitation, stepped inside the room and closed the door to behind me.

Now my heart was thumping and my breathing short and more rapid than normal. It reminded me of times as a boy when I'd been scrumping for apples with my two best friends, none of us wanting to admit that we were frightened to death, all the while struggling to keep control of nerves that left us almost incapable of movement. I decided that if I, at least initially, remained with my back to the surgery door then I would have the best possible opportunity of hearing footsteps on the stairs. What evasive action I might be able to take in order to avoid detection, I had not the slightest idea.

The room was large; larger than I had been expecting. It was of roughly the same proportions as the dining room, though nowhere near as heavily furnished. My eye was caught almost at once by the sight of a sizeable leather chair, a reclining one, of the sort you expect to see in such a surgery. It looked almost new, the fine, dark leather hardly marked or scored, except for a number of creases in the middle of the lower section where a person would sit. Alongside that was a plain leather armchair, again one that looked almost new. It was clear that one would be occupied by Sneijder.

To my right was a substantial dark wooden sideboard, on the top of which sat a vase of dried flowers, the somewhat spice-like smell of which permeated the room. To my left was an enormous oak desk and a fireplace. I had an almost overwhelming urge to explore the desk, but fear of being caught where I should not be held me back. In truth, I struggled to properly understand my presence in the room and certainly would not have been able to justify it. The concerns that I felt were real to me but, as for evidence to support them, that would be difficult to present in my defence, should the need arise.

From my vantage point by the door, the room seemed perfectly normal for a Doctor's surgery and I chided myself for such stupid behaviour. All the same, something within me continued to nag away and I looked again at the desk. No longer able to resist and my heart now thumping in my chest, I walked straight across the room, around to the far side of the Doctor's desk and set about testing each drawer in turn. None would give. Sneijder kept them all locked.

Now I was loose in the room, there seemed to be no stopping me. I sprung back across the surgery and set about the sideboard, only to find it contained nothing more interesting than an eye mask, of the sort you use when having trouble sleeping, a pair of small towels and a stock of unused notepads. I felt wholly disappointed, though why, I could not say. It seemed that a part of me wanted or, perhaps, expected to find something more unusual or alarming.

But it was not the time to dwell on such disappointments. I had already tested my luck in the extreme and so made my way back to the door without further delay. It is difficult to listen properly for faint, distant sounds when your heart is thumping and your breathing is irregular and I was by no means certain the coast was clear as I eased the door ajar, but I found no one there and slipped away as quietly and carefully as I had arrived.

It was as I sat back down in the sitting room chair I had occupied before my little excursion that I noticed Scurry was no longer there. A dreadful thought that he might have seen me sneaking into the Doctor's surgery swept over me, but there was nothing to be done. No doubt if he had seen me and had something to say on the matter then he would do so in good time. Annoyed at myself for such carelessness, I picked up the book I had been reading previously and made out I was engrossed once more as I replayed in my mind's eye my visit to Sneijder's surgery, wondering above all else why I felt quite such an overwhelming sense of unease. Was I being overcome by paranoia, perhaps brought on by boredom, or was there really something terribly wrong going on here?

A MAN OF HONOUR

After lunch, at which I ate alone with Sneijder, I tried once more to take a turn in the garden, but was quickly forced back into the house by the persisting fog and returned to my room to rest on my bed for a half hour or so, not tired enough to sleep. Afterwards, I once more found myself confined to the sitting room, where I took to drawing strange creatures that I imagined might appear out of the fog in the middle of the darkest of nights. Unhappily, my attempts were rather poor.

Around three, Sneijder stopped by to say that he believed it possible the fog may start to thin out later in the day. The housekeeper was a local woman, he informed me, and she was of the opinion a wind was sure to blow in soon, though on what she based such a view, Sneijder did not say. He seemed a little agitated, not wanting to linger for conversation, and for the first time since my arrival I got the impression he wished me gone as soon as possible; a view underlined by his statement that Selkman was available to take me back to New Cumnock as soon as the weather allowed. Had he, I wondered, worked out that I had been into his surgery? Perhaps there was some item I had unintentionally disturbed that gave away my actions. I chose to ignore the thought and pushed it to the back of my mind, though not without some difficulty.

It was a little after Sneijder's visit, at a time when I knew him to be in his surgery with Harold Duncan, that Elizabeth Fitzsimon joined me in the sitting room. She was in a distressed state, lines of worry etched into her pretty face and her hands almost constantly on the move, unable to rest for anything but the briefest of moments. Something was clearly wrong, that much I could tell, before she had started relating what she had come to say. When she did speak, her voice was faltering, the confusion that must have been whirling through her mind making itself apparent in her struggle to put together coherent sentences. Not altogether surprisingly, she seemed a little uncertain how honest she might be with me, but a degree of desperation appeared to push her on.

"Mr Templeman… I… I…"

"Do take a seat, Miss Fitzsimon. You look rather distressed."

She shook her head and closed her eyes for a moment. "No. I can't."

I stood up and placed a hand gently on her right forearm. "Perhaps a few deep breaths will help."

She nodded, then filled her lungs with air, holding it there a little longer than would be usual, before letting it back out. She repeated this exercise twice more and it did, indeed, appear to calm her a little.

"Now then, how can I help you?" I asked, taking my hand from her arm.

"I hope you won't think me mad, Mr Templeman." She held a hand to her mouth and for a second or two closed her eyes again. "Oh, dear. I don't know who else I can turn to. We're so isolated here and there's so little chance of reaching anyone else."

"I can assure you, Miss Fitzsimon, I won't think you in

the least bit mad. In fact, you seem perfectly sane to me."

To say that I was intrigued would be something of an understatement. I was most anxious to hear what she had to say and realised that my entire body had tensed, like a cat waiting to pounce. It was an odd sensation, there, at that time, but into my head returned my own earlier feelings of how peculiar things seemed to be in this house, most especially the patients.

"Mr Templeman, I… I believe that Doctor Sneijder is attempting to manipulate me. To fix unreasonable and undesirable thoughts in my mind."

She looked close to tears as she spoke and I could see that she had begun to shake. I considered my response carefully, conscious that she was there because her father believed she was in need of specialist help with her mental and emotional state.

"That is quite a serious claim. Do you mind if I ask why you think he's doing that?"

"He uses hypnosis. He sits us down in that big chair in his surgery and uses his pocket watch, swinging on its chain, to hypnotise us. I don't seem to be very susceptible to the practice and twice he has been unsuccessful in hypnotising me. On both occasions he didn't at first notice and proceeded with his treatment as if I was under his control."

She paused and took another deep breath. I looked around, along the hallway, anxious to avoid our exchange being overheard and wishing to have the opportunity to take action if someone should be seen approaching. For now we were, as far as I could tell, entirely alone.

"What is it he says to you when this happens that gives you such cause for concern?"

"He asks me to think about how terrible a thing war is. How awful it would be if members of my family were to be killed or seriously maimed as a result of fighting in a war. Then he goes on to suggest that Great Britain should not oppose Germany and its allies if there should be another war on the Continent. He tells me that I should do all I can to persuade my father to the same point of view."

I was taken aback. Whatever I might have suspected, it would never have been this. My mind raced, trying all at once to piece together the possibility of a diabolical scheme, but I forced myself to set that aside and focus on Miss Fitzsimon.

"And was it at this point that he realised you weren't hypnotised?"

"Yes, the first time I opened my eyes with alarm. I think he was shocked to see me still far from under his spell. The second time he said he could tell I was not under because of my eye movements. When I challenged him, he said he was merely doing his part to help ensure peace continued in Europe. But the look in his eyes, Mr Templeman. That didn't suggest he was sincere about wanting peace. He looked more as if he was frustrated, angry even. I've been so afraid. Too scared to say anything else to Doctor Sneijder and there seems to be no way of reaching help on my own when we are so isolated here."

She looked by now close to collapse and I tried once more to persuade her to sit down, but she again refused.

"Well, you did the right thing to confide in me, Miss Fitzsimon. You don't need to have any concerns there. In truth, I've thought things a little odd here since I recovered from my concussion. As a matter of fact, I had even wondered if my concussion was still affecting my senses."

Much of the tension that had filled Miss Fitzsimon's body seemed at this point to leave her. She let out a long sigh and a little brightness returned to her eyes.

"I can't tell you how happy I am to hear you say that, Mr Templeman. I couldn't be certain it was safe to speak to you, not at first. I thought you might perhaps be an associate of the Doctor, or even a patient yourself."

"I suppose I was a patient for a while, though not of the

same sort as the rest of you. Have you not been able to speak to any of the other patients about your concerns? Perhaps to establish if they have been subjected to the same treatment as yourself?"

"No. I did try speaking to Mrs Downing, but I think the Doctor has her fully under his spell." She hesitated for a moment, before continuing, "You don't think I'm imagining things, do you? I'm not really going mad?"

She sounded a little uncertain, as if she couldn't quite believe herself, no doubt the result of Sneijder's efforts to persuade her that she really did have emotional problems. I suppose I ought to have been more cautious and considered fully this possibility; after all, I was no medical Doctor and it was entirely possible I was being hoodwinked by a patient suffering from paranoia, but what she had told me so matched my own sense of unease and suspicion that I couldn't stop myself from taking her at her word.

I don't suppose we had been talking for more than three or four minutes, but I had, all the same, been careless. Looking up towards the doorway, I saw standing there the figure of Sneijder and the huge, bulking presence of Selkman behind him. Sneijder wore an expression that would have better suited the worst of criminals in an overly melodramatic stage play, his eyes fixed on me, sharp as bayonets, and his eyebrows lowered. When he spoke there was an insistent, almost threatening tone to his words. It unnerved me for a moment.

"You really should not believe what Miss Fitzsimon tells you, Mr Templeman. She is suffering from an acute emotional disorder that includes displays of paranoia and fantasised storytelling. She is a young woman who needs help. Help of the sort only an expert such as I can provide, not a layman."

The last few words were, of course, aimed full square at me. Sneijder was attempting to put me firmly in my place, that much was obvious. I was unimpressed.

"I think, Doctor, that Miss Fitzsimon should be free to make up her own mind as to what is good for her and what is not."

I had no intention of abandoning Miss Fitzsimon without putting up a fight. The moral ground was ours, despite Sneijder's insistence that it was a matter for him and him alone. I may have been quivering with nerves, but this was no time for weakness.

My assertiveness was too much for Sneijder, who wasted no more time on a diplomatic approach. Although he remained fully in control of himself, the flare of his nostrils and the narrowing of his eyes made it clear he was determined to have his way. His words were now a command. "Mr Templeman, you will return to your room and remain there."

I felt Miss Fitzsimon move across and behind me, clearly anxious to keep me between herself and Sneijder. I didn't need to be a Doctor to realise the woman was afraid. Anger began to well up inside me at the Doctor's rude insistence, fuelled by my growing conviction that it was he who was engaging in fantasies, not his terrified patient. I stood my ground and wrapped an arm around behind me as a shield for Miss Fitzsimon.

"No, Doctor, I will not. I insist that we contact Sir Eustace at once and ask him to hear what his daughter has to say. If you won't allow that, then I'll speak to him myself."

There was a brief pause before Sneijder gestured with a wave of the hand for Selkman to move forward.

"No, Templeman, you will do nothing of the sort. I won't have you or anyone else interfering in a patient's treatment. It could lead to complications, possibly permanent damage. Selkman, escort Mr Templeman to his room and make sure he does not leave it until I say he can."

I prepared to square up to the imposing bulk of the

Doctor's handyman, but just as my fate seemed to be sealed and I feared coming off considerably the worse, Elizabeth Fitzsimon stepped out from behind me.

"No, please, there's no need. Doctor Sneijder is right. I'm… I'm just tired and overwrought." As she looked at me there was a sad, piteous tone in her voice and tears in the corners of her eyes.

"But..."

"No, Mr Templeman, really, you must listen to Doctor Sneijder." She sounded as though she was pleading with me and I found it hard not to respond in the way I thought I should, but something about the way she looked suggested she was not giving up, merely making a tactical retreat.

I looked again at Sneijder, then Selkman and finally back to the upset patient. I trusted to my instincts. "Well, if you're certain, Miss Fitzsimon."

She nodded once, then let her gaze fall to the floor.

Selkman took me by the arm. I shrugged him off.

"We will speak later, Mr Templeman."

With those last words from Sneijder, I was escorted by the silent Selkman along the hallway and up the stairs to my bedroom, the whole time wondering what I should do next, frustrated by the outcome in the sitting room. Leaving Elizabeth Fitzsimon alone with the Doctor, as I had, left me feeling annoyed and, frankly, something of a coward.

Those were my thoughts as Selkman closed the door on me and I continued turning them over in my mind for some little while as I stared out of the window, wishing to God that the fog would begin to lift soon. On one thing I was clear: as soon as I could see where I was going, I would leave the house, on foot if I had to, find whatever help I could and return at once to the house. What Miss Fitzsimon had told me was alarming in the extreme.

For some reason, I know not why, I thought to try the door to my room. When I did, I found it was locked from the outside. I was, at least for the time being, a prisoner.

A BID FOR FREEDOM

I must admit to being somewhat shocked at finding I was locked in my room, as if I were a common criminal confined to a cell. Worse followed when I tried the window and found it would not open more than a few inches and certainly not enough to allow me to escape the room that way, even if I were not already put off by the considerable drop to the ground.

Unable to have any direct impact on events, I paced my room in frustration, reviewing the situation in an attempt to come up with a clear plan of action. In truth, I was still somewhat perplexed as to quite what my situation actually was. Whilst it was clear enough that something was wrong and Elizabeth Fitzsimon had come across as a perfectly sane and lucid woman, I simply could not fathom what a Dutch Doctor was doing in Great Britain attempting to persuade or, as his upset and frightened patient had put it, indoctrinate people into thinking that a possible war with Germany, if it came to that, should be opposed and avoided.

After spending a fruitless quarter of an hour attempting to unravel the Doctor's motives and the claims and counter claims made by him and Miss Fitzsimon, I slumped into the tatty armchair by the window and, I must admit, fell into a deep slump, thinking my position hopeless. It was at this point that I heard a key inserted into the lock of the door and turned. I was barely on my feet, determined to demand my freedom, when the door opened and Sneijder stepped into the room.

I hurled my frustrations at him without a moment's thought. "How dare you lock me in this room. I demand my freedom at once. Right now. And I insist on speaking to Miss Fitzsimon again. You've absolutely no right to keep me under lock and key."

My huffing and puffing appeared to have little effect on Sneijder, who responded in a dismissive tone, underlined with a backward wave of his right hand. "Quiet, Templeman. I've had enough of you already. I should have left you to rot on the driveway and saved myself the considerable trouble you have brought to this otherwise happy house."

"Happy?" I took a step towards him. "How in God's name can you say happy? Did Miss Fitzsimon appear happy to you?"

"I said quiet." It was a command this time and, as if to underline the fact, Selkman stepped forward to show himself on the landing.

Sneijder adjusted his cuffs and took a deep breath, avoiding, for the moment, any further eye contact with me. I assumed he was composing himself prior to telling me whatever it was he had come to say. Whatever it was to be, I felt disinclined to believe him.

"It has taken me much effort, Mr Templeman, to calm down Miss Fitzsimon. The poor woman was distraught, a situation not in the least bit helped by your interference. I have instructed Selkman that, as soon as there is even the smallest break in the fog, he is to take you back to New Cumnock without delay, forcibly if needs be, though I hope you will go along without fuss. In the meantime, I simply cannot take the chance that you will upset another of the patients, so you will remain confined to this room. Mrs Rafferty will bring you food and drink for so long as you remain with us. Let us hope it is not long."

I am not sure what I was expecting from Sneijder. An apology perhaps. Maybe an explanation that might enlighten me as to Miss Fitzsimon's unsettled state of mind. As it turned out, his words were like a red rag to a bull.

"By God, Sneijder, you are not my gaoler. I insist on being given back my freedom. What kind of place are you running here? Why was Miss Fitzsimon so upset and what are you hiding? I won't..."

"Enough." Sneijder bellowed, his face tinged red and his eyes bright with rage. "You will remain here and you will leave when Selkman tells you to do so. This matter is not open to discussion."

With that, he turned on his heels and stalked out of the room. Selkman lingered for a moment, eyeing me in that same, now all-too-familiar, dumb way that he had done from the start. Whatever it was that was playing through his mind, I had not the least idea and very little desire to find out. When the time came to leave, I could see little point in attempting to delay the process. He was perfectly capable of swatting me like a fly.

*

As Selkman closed and locked the door to my room once more, I threw back my head and puffed out my cheeks. Finding myself entirely unable to influence events, or do anything at all to change my situation, was not only frustrating, it also left me feeling somewhat inadequate and inept. I chastised myself for making the mistake of giving vent to my feelings and throwing demands at Sneijder when, I began to see, it might have proved far more effective to have taken a conciliatory approach. If I had, perhaps, been able to put his mind at ease and bring him round to believing that I represented no threat to whatever it was he was engaged in, then he might have had second thoughts and taken a chance on releasing me from my room. At least then I would have been in a position where I could attempt to find out more about Sneijder's activities. Instead, I was stuck, unable to see, hear or do anything.

This was my mental state for some while, alternating between self-chastisement, frustration and anger, in equal measure, until I once more heard a key inserted into the lock of the door. And then, entirely out of the blue, an idea came to me; a possible way out of my prison.

I was at the time sitting on the edge of the bed, swinging my feet to and fro. Quickly jumping up, I grabbed hold of the wash bowl that was set in a wooden stand in the corner of the room nearest to me and sat back down with it in my lap. Nursing it with both hands and leaning my head over the bowl, I began to groan and retch, as if suffering from some hideous illness, all the while looking to the left, out the side of my eye, as the door swung open. As it did so, I saw the housekeeper walk in, carrying a tray, on which was set a tea service and some fruit. The woman's face was as unwelcoming and sour as ever, which pleased me, because I might have felt a pang of guilt at what I was about to do had she been in a more cheerful mood.

She saw me at once, stopped, stared, then, without a word, turned and walked across to the cabinet in front of the window, so she could set down the tray. I continued to groan and act as if I was about to be violently ill, while, at the same time, I began to set my body for what I had in mind. I don't deny there was something of a thrill about the affair; an excitement at such a daring deed and, I hoped, the return of my freedom.

I was anxious that she should not easily see my face, for fear it might be all too obvious I was not in the least bit unwell. If that should happen, my plans were sure to unravel swiftly. As she drew closer and the stale smell of her grew stronger, I all but buried my nose in the empty bowl and began to cough extravagantly. She paused for a moment, seemingly thinking it might be best to hold back until I had somewhat recovered myself, then stepped closer still, peering down and moving her head a little from side to side in an attempt to see my face more clearly.

"I'll get you some water," she uttered in an almost incomprehensible mumble that offered no sign of concern or sympathy.

As she turned to walk back to the other side of the room, I leapt up off the bed in one bound, filled my lungs with air, then, in one smooth action, swept the bowl up to somewhere just above my shoulders and brought it down as hard as I could as I closed to within an arm's length of her. It shattered in an explosion of Lord knows how many pieces as it made contact with her head and my fingers were left grasping nothing but air. Just managing to stop myself from toppling over as my body weight shifted forward behind the terrible blow, I watched the housekeeper stagger, wobble, then collapse to the floor, as if she had not a single bone in her body.

My fingers were tingling from the force of the blow and my head pounding as my heart beat madly. I was exhilarated. There is no other way to put it, such was my sense of excitement at what I had just done. But there was also an edge of fear now over what I had started and the knowledge that there was no going back, no means of trying to explain away my assault as some sort of unfortunate accident. I was committed to a course of action, with no guarantee of success and no real idea of the consequences of failure, other than they would not be good. If Sneijder had chosen to lock me up for such a minor offence as I had given him so far, what he might be capable of should he apprehend me before I could make good my escape was not worth thinking about. I clenched my fists and drove the feelings of fear and inadequacy to the back of my mind.

Pausing only to confirm I had done no more than knock out the housekeeper, I stole across the room to the still open door and paused so as to listen before attempting to proceed further. I was greeted by the welcome sound of deafening silence, which gave me confidence to peer out onto the landing. There was no sign of Selkman, the one member of the household who provoked real fear in me, given his immense size and strength.

Since my scheme had begun on an impulse, entirely opportunistic in nature, I had no definite plan in mind for what I was to do next, other than a general desire to leave the house as quickly as possible. But it occurred to me, there and then, that perhaps I ought to attempt to take Miss Fitzsimon with me. True, she might find the journey a challenging one but, in her favour, she was young and without physical impediment, as far as I was aware. There was also the possibility that she might suffer further at the hands of Sneijder if I was to leave her there, even if it was only for as long as it took me to bring help.

With this thought fresh in my mind, I stepped out onto the landing and walked with the greatest care towards the stairs, constantly searching for sounds that would warn me someone was approaching. My palms were moist with sweat and every muscle in my body seemed to be tensioned like a spring. Still the blood beat in my head like a drum, while my throat had begun to feel dry and taut. Was I the hunter or the hunted? I must admit, I could not distinguish between the two at that point.

As I reached the top of the stairs, I heard voices from somewhere downstairs. I stopped at once, rooted to the spot, and listened some more, straining to make out who was talking and where they were. There it was again. A man's voice. Then a second, another man. I couldn't make out who was speaking, but I could tell they were in Sneijder's surgery. I peered over the banister with care. The door to the surgery was, indeed, closed. But dare I risk continuing when there was a possibility someone would leave the room before I managed to get down the stairs and away?

I dithered, too afraid to proceed, arguing with myself whether to move or not. This procrastination turned out to be fortunate because the surgery door opened, only partially at first, then, after more discussion between the two men, all the way. Harold Duncan stepped out and proceeded to walk off down the hallway and out of my sight.

I waited, half-expecting Sneijder to come next, but instead the door closed and I was, it seemed, once more on my own and free to proceed. My nerve was, however, at risk of deserting me at a key moment; my hands were trembling a little and it took much effort to persuade myself to take the first step on to the stairs.

It was a horrible experience making my way down those stairs. I felt awfully exposed and with each step I fully expected the timbers to creak or squeal as they took my weight, giving away my approach to the entire house. Indeed, I imagined in my nervousness that any such noise was bound to reach such a terrible pitch it would be capable of waking all but the dead. By the time I reached the last step, still as yet undetected, my legs were stiff with cramp, which I could only put down to the enormous tension running through me.

My mind was still confused as to whether or not I should search for Miss Fitzsimon in the hope of taking her with me and, yet again, I hesitated as to what to do next. My inept performance and inability to make a clear-cut decision began to gnaw at my already limited confidence and I started to wonder if I was even up to the task of walking away from the house, simple though such a thing ought to have been.

As I attempted to bring a degree of calmness to my mind, so that I might make a considered and rational decision, I heard once more voices coming from the surgery. This I had not expected, having assumed that only Sneijder and Duncan would have been in the room; clearly I was wrong about that. There were two voices and they were both male. One did most of the talking by far and was without question Sneijder, but the other spoke only a little and I could not make out who it was.

In an attempt to hear more clearly I brought myself up close to the door and pressed my left ear against the timber. So anxious was I not to give myself away that I realised, after a short while, that I had, for the moment, forgone the small matter of breathing and was forced all of a sudden to take a long, deep breath. Fortunately, it did not attract the attention of anyone inside the room.

As I focused once more on the matter in hand and attuned my hearing to the conversation inside the surgery, it seemed I had arrived at a most opportune moment. Sneijder was speaking.

"I will bring Miss Fitzsimon in for another session in half an hour. We will need to speed up her processing now, after that little outburst of hers. It is regrettable that she is not so easily hypnotised as most, but I have encountered people like her before and almost all respond sooner or later. Mrs Downing, on the other hand, has progressed most satisfactorily and she will be able to leave as planned in two days. I have every confidence she will continue to vouch for our masters."

The other man spoke, only a few words, but I could make out none of them. Then Sneijder, who must have moved to a different spot in the room because his voice came from further to my left, spoke again.

"Now then, your biggest priority, Selkman, is to keep an eye on Mr Templeman and make absolutely sure he does not leave his room until it is time for you to take him back to New Cumnock. His suspicions have already been aroused and I am not altogether convinced I have persuaded him that Miss Fitzsimon was being nothing more than a little hysterical. If he manages to do any more snooping around, I fear he might well uncover the real purpose of our work here and that we cannot afford. There is too much more to be done to be packing up and returning to Germany just yet."

This time I could just make out Selkman's response. It was brief, no more than a confirmation of his orders. I was, however, stunned and remained frozen to the spot. Germany? Their real purpose? What had I stumbled upon? I had thought Sneijder was perhaps engaging in methods of treatment that could quite possibly be detrimental to his patients and attract the displeasure of his profession. I also considered his behaviour towards me and Miss Fitzsimon to be entirely unacceptable, but that was as far as my suspicions had taken me.

A plethora of thoughts began to flit through my mind as I tried to piece together a coherent picture, incredulous at what I had just heard, but I was shaken out of my thoughts by the sound of approaching footsteps on the wooden floor of the surgery. Never had I been so afraid of discovery as I was then and I felt my whole body tense once again. But just when it looked like I was sure to be discovered and apprehended for a second time, the footsteps stopped and Sneijder spoke again.

"You'd better bring in some more firewood and see if there aren't any signs of the fog beginning to thin. It can't go on for much longer, surely to God."

Selkman acknowledged his latest orders before Sneijder spoke further.

"Once I've written up my notes on Harold Duncan, I

shall speak to Mrs Rafferty to see how our prisoner is getting along. Then I believe it will be time for lunch."

Before the Doctor had finished speaking, I had already decided on two things. One was that I would indeed attempt to take Elizabeth Fitzsimon with me when I left the house in search of help. The other, which I set about putting into action at once, was to make my way down the side of the stairs as quickly and silently as possible to the cellar door, which, to my relief, I found unlocked. I opened it, stepped inside and closed the door just as I heard the door to the surgery open. My heart was racing, but I felt an overwhelming sense of relief at reaching safety.

Footsteps, slow and heavy as only those of Selkman could be, passed along the hallway and off towards the sitting room. Waiting until I was as sure as I could be that Selkman was nowhere to be seen, I eased open the cellar door and peered through the crack I had made for myself. Nothing was to be seen or heard. Slipping back into the hallway, I followed in Selkman's footsteps, hoping that I might be lucky enough to find Miss Fitzsimon in one of the downstairs rooms. The thought of having to go back up the stairs in search of her was not an appealing one.

The sitting room was empty, so I pressed on towards the dining room, feeling increasingly confident in my abilities to evade being discovered, since the housekeeper was flat out on the bedroom floor, unconscious, Sneijder was busy in his surgery and Selkman was chopping firewood outside. Therefore, when I found the dining room was occupied only by Harold Duncan, who chose to ignore me entirely, I was able, with only a little difficulty, to persuade myself to head upstairs and so I turned to make my way back along the hallway.

It was as I reached the door from the sitting room to the hallway that the front door opened. I had no time to think, for Selkman walked straight into the house. I could not believe my eyes at first. What was he doing there, rather than coming back in through the rear entrance, having made his way in through the kitchen. I shook my head, but there he was. Not only that, but he was now looking directly at me and, for the first time, I saw him smile, or at least something akin to a smile appeared on his face. It was rather more like a sickening smirk of delight. He turned and began to stomp towards me, much faster than I thought him capable of moving. I glanced quickly left then right, but finding nothing by way of a weapon and Selkman already so close that he was beginning to darken the hallway, I made an instant decision to take the attack to him, hoping I might catch him off guard. After all, why would he expect such an ordinary and ill-equipped man such as me to go hand-to-hand with a giant like him.

My heart pumped madly and my mind cleared of all other thoughts than securing my own safety and survival. I hurled myself towards him, my fists clenched and mouth open, some gibberish of a war cry rising up from within me. I smashed into him, landing solid punches into both his flanks, wondering if I might get lucky and hit a kidney; something I vaguely recalled from a boy's story book was supposed to be effective in putting down an opponent, however enormous they might be.

My efforts must have seemed feeble, for the giant of a man did not appear to even flinch. Meanwhile, the air burst out of my lungs all at once upon the impact and I had to draw deeply to refill them. There was still that same unpleasant smirk on Selkman's face, so I aimed a blow, a raking upper cut, as powerfully as I could manage, at his rock-like chin. But he blocked it with ease, knocking away my arm with a flick of one hand. I stumbled, working hard to maintain my balance, but the initiative was now with him and he used it at once by attempting to grab hold of my jacket with one of his huge hands. Pulling back just in the nick of time, I evaded his reach and swayed to my left, hoping I could outflank him and land a blow to his ribs.

Again Selkman lunged at me with with an outstretched hand, which I this time deflected sufficiently with a downward cut of my right fist to make him pull back. I was aware by now of nothing apart from the two of us, the rest of the world an indistinguishable blur on the edge of my vision, and already my lungs were in need of more oxygen, as my breathing had become short and shallow.

Then a thought came to me to try something different. If I couldn't land an effective blow to his upper body or his face using my fists, then I might manage to deliver one elsewhere using my feet. I stepped forward once more to close the gap between us, made as if to land a punch to his chin, then struck out with my right foot, aiming for his left shin with the point of my shoe.

But he was too good a fighter to fall for my feint and more nimble than I would have hoped. Evading my kick, he stepped to his right and a bludgeoning right hook arced high up over his shoulder and down towards me. Oddly, I seemed to be able to see it coming for an extraordinarily long time, but was entirely unable to take any kind of evasive action and, as it hit the side of my face, it sent a shuddering wave of excruciating pain through my entire body. The last thing I can recall is the feeling of my knees buckling as I collapsed to the floor.

A CELL OF MY OWN

It seemed at first as if I was trapped in a perpetual night-time of total darkness. I thought I had opened my eyes sufficiently to see the world around me, but, when there was nothing to be seen, I bit back the pain and slowly eased them open as fully as I could manage. But still the world remained in total darkness. A terrible, irrational fear came over me in a moment, the notion that I had in fact died under the powerful blows of Selkman and now lay in some intermediate zone of darkness, a void if you like, between the one world and the next, awaiting my fate of Heaven or Hell.

Trembling at the thought and filled in an instant with remorse and regret, afraid that I might have failed to live to a sufficient degree the life of an upstanding God-fearing, loving and forgiving man, I cried out within at the possibility I might be destined for the underworld. If only I could live my life again, I wouldn't repeat those mistakes that may have marked me down as unworthy of ascending to Paradise. But I couldn't do any such thing, of course, for my days were done and it was the time of reckoning.

Tears began to form under my eyelids, so wretched did

I feel, but as the very worst of thoughts were consuming me like a raging fire does a new, dried log, deliverance was presented to me. As my eyes adjusted to my new situation, they were able to make out slivers of light from somewhere up above me. As I struggled to focus in on the light, it grew brighter and clearer, until I was able, at last, to make out what it was. Away and up to my right there was a door and the light I could see was penetrating the gap between the door itself and its frame. It wasn't much, but it was enough.

A prayer of gratitude left my lips; A heartfelt thanks for being given another chance. Never had I felt so close to my God as I did then. I was a young, headstrong, fool who had very nearly thrown away his life with hardly a decent thing to show for it. My sense of relief was immense.

I reached out tentatively around me with both hands, for I had by now realised that I was laid out on a floor which was, I discovered, nothing other than cold, damp earth. That and the position of the doorway above me suggested only one thing, that I was in the cellar of the Doctor's house. A natural enough place to incarcerate me, I supposed, seeing as I had managed to escape from the locked bedroom.

Wanting to investigate further, I then attempted to sit up, but had barely raised my head from the ground than the left side of my face started to throb and burn. A terrible headache hit me with such force that I felt instantly sick. Unable to compose myself, I eased my head back to the ground, hoping the pain would abate and the sickness leave me, but instead I started to feel light-headed and was glad not to be on my feet. I closed my eyes and tried to persuade my mind and body that the pain wasn't real, just a figment of my imagination, and, in a moment or two, I was unconscious once more.

*

It was the shaking that awoke me. Rough and unforgiving, it moved my whole body from side to side, as if I was a rag doll. I wished it would stop, for the violent movements made my headache all the worse and did little for the pain that seared the side of my face. As I came to, feeling groggy and stiff from the cold, I began to hear a voice somewhere close by. At first, all I could make out were two or three words here and there and it took me a little while to regain my senses and start to understand what was being said.

Big powerful hands gripped me under the armpits and pulled me upright, into a seated position, then dragged me backwards until I was loosely propped up against a damp wall. Every muscle in my body seemed to ache, my mouth was dry as the Sahara Desert and I found it hard to focus. The room had become an unstable blur and there was a strong smell of decay and damp in my nostrils that made me shiver a little.

"Templeman! Can you hear me?" The voice was commanding and unmistakeable. So close I could hardly fail to recognise it as that of Sneijder, even through my weakened state. "Selkman," he barked. The giant grabbed my right shoulder and shook me aggressively.

"All right," I mumbled through my dry lips. "Enough."

"Water, Selkman."

The henchman held a glass to my lips and pushed my head back, so that my mouth opened. It was all I could do not to choke on the cool, fresh water as it poured into my mouth and, welcome though it was, I had to put a hand up to indicate I'd had enough for the time being.

"You can hear me properly now, Templeman?" asked Sneijder.

"Yes." I nodded weakly, immediately regretting the effort, as it was rewarded with yet more pain in my head.

"Good, then I can make myself clear." Sneijder was

standing alongside me, completing a pincer movement with Selkman, who remained in place to my right. There cannot have been any light fittings in the room, for Sneijder held a torch, which he ran up and down the length of me twice, no doubt assessing my condition. "You have been a considerable problem to me since we found you lying on our driveway, Mr Templeman. I have expended time and energy attending to your injuries, provided you with food and lodging when there was no compunction upon me to do so and, until recently, given you almost a free run of the house. And how have you repaid me, Mr Templeman?"

I tried to speak, but instead began to cough. Selkman returned with the glass of water and I drank from it again, eking out every possible second so that I could continue to recover my senses. Sneijder flashed the torch in my eyes, causing me to turn away and raise a hand in front of my face.

"I will tell you how you have repaid my hospitality, Mr Templeman. You have upset my patients and interfered with their treatment. You have attacked and knocked unconscious my housekeeper and you have assaulted Selkman here; more fool you."

Sneijder paused. I wasn't sure if it was for my benefit, so that I might better keep up with what I was being told, or for Sneijder to consider his next words before delivering them.

"Well, I can assure you now that your interference in my work here is at an end. I simply will not tolerate any more meddling from you." There was anger in his voice and the beam from the torch wobbled in all directions as his hand shook with fury. "You will now remain here in the cellar until our work is complete. And you should be under no illusions, Templeman, should you attempt another escape you can expect to be shot, dead if necessary. Do I make myself clear?"

I was, for a moment, somewhat taken aback by the nature of his threat. Did he really expect me to believe that he would shoot a man dead, in cold blood? I looked at him hard, trying to focus my eyes fully, in an attempt to better assess his intentions, but a combination of the almost non-existent lighting and my muddled head meant that I could hardly make out much of the man at all.

"I know what you are doing, Sneijder," I muttered, my brain not quite able to communicate with my mouth properly.

"Do you indeed? Did you hear that, Selkman? He knows what we are doing. I wonder what on Earth he can mean?" The sarcasm in Sneijder's words was difficult to miss. "You're a fool, Templeman. What do you think you can do against the three of us in this isolated spot, miles from anywhere and lost in a fog so thick you cannot see beyond the end of your nose?" He laughed, but without mirth.

"You won't get..." I started, but winced with pain and gasped out loud as Sneijder landed a well-placed kick in the side of my left knee. Like any good Doctor, he knew where to find exposed and effective points of pain.

"There is no need for you to talk, Templeman. We are not interested in what you have to say. You English are all the same. You think you are so superior to everyone else. God's chosen ones. Well, there is a new power rising, Mr Templeman, and not even the decaying, corrupt British Empire will stop it from achieving its rightful place in the world."

"So, you are German?"

"Of course, I'm German, though I think I have done a most commendable job passing myself off as a Hollander. It took quite a lot of training to get the accent right and I spent more hours than I care to recall learning about my supposed homeland, in case anyone should be impolite enough to start asking many questions."

"You expect war then, I take it?" I rubbed my knee, wondering how much more pain I could expect to suffer.

"Indeed, war is inevitable. If not this year, then next. And if not next, then the year after. But war will come and we will be ready for it, better prepared and better equipped than anyone else. And if I have anything to do with things, then your British Government will choose to stay out, though it does not matter if my efforts fall short, for the outcome of the fighting will be the same."

I wanted to object, to fight our nation's corner, but my growing anger only served to make my confusion and blurred thinking worse and the words would not come. As I struggled for something to say, I watched Sneijder bend down to pick up his Doctor's bag, open it and lift out a needle. He nodded towards Selkman, who bent over me, that horribly familiar smirk inches from my face, and pinned my arms to my sides. Filling the needle with a clear liquid from a small bottle, Sneijder ordered Selkman to roll up my left sleeve, which he did with ease, despite my efforts to resist.

"Poison, is it, Sneijder?" It was more of an accusation than a question, for all the difference it made.

"Poison? Don't be a fool, Templeman. That would leave evidence that could find its way back to us. No, we have other plans for you. It seems that you never did make it to the safety of this house and instead got lost on the hills, there to die of exposure; although I am sure leaving you tied up in the garden overnight will achieve the same outcome. Then Selkman will carry you to some nearby hillside and leave you there with the sheep. Someone will find your body, eventually." He jabbed the needle into my arm and I felt the fluid being pumped into my veins. "This will merely ensure you remain asleep for a while. A sleeping man will be no further trouble to us."

"You'll regret this, Sneijder." I think I must have repeated those words over and over again, more and more feebly each time, as I slipped away once more into unconsciousness.

NO HOPE FOR THE FUTURE

The injection Sneijder administered caused me to sleep for a little over six hours, according to my pocket watch. When I came to, I once more felt groggy and disorientated, not sure where I was or why everything was so dark. As I pulled myself slowly into a sitting position, my back against a stone wall, I took stock of my physical and mental condition.

Whilst further exposure to the damp and the cold did nothing to make me feel any better, the long, uninterrupted sleep had at least given my body time to recover somewhat from the blows it had taken during my fight with Selkman. For one thing, the side of my face throbbed a little less, though it was still somewhat sore. It seemed any other knocks and blows I had suffered were of no real concern; certainly not enough to interfere in any renewed escape attempt I might choose to undertake.

My mental state, on the other hand, was less certain. Indeed, I would even go so far as to say that, without some attention and improvement, there was every possibility it would put an end to any further initiatives on my part, even before they had begun. I was in a poor way. For one thing, the effects of the sleeping drug that Sneijder had given me were slow to wear off and I was finding it hard to concentrate and bring my thoughts together, which was less than ideal given my situation. At least it seemed likely, given a little more time, those effects would subside. There again, just how much time remained for me I could not say and there was also the possibility Sneijder would return to inject me a second time. That was an unpleasant thought.

I realised too that my self-esteem and confidence had taken a considerable knock. Whilst I would never have described myself as the heroic type, nor recognised in me a man with the build and skills to see off all comers in a fist fight, I had considered myself a fit and healthy specimen of manhood, with a sharp brain that stood me in good stead in whatever difficult situation I might face.

Recent events, however, had shown all this to be nothing more than fancy on my own part. I had been found to possess neither the physical prowess to fight off my oppressors, with the exception of the housekeeper I had shamelessly smashed over the head with a washing bowl, nor the mental dexterity and clarity of purpose to outwit them. In fact, I had made a stupid mistake in choosing to search for Miss Fitzsimon rather than escaping the house when the opportunity was there to be taken. It was that shortcoming that had resulted in my being locked in the cellar. What good was I as a rescuer of the Doctor's victims when I lay there, incarcerated and with little opportunity of escape?

I felt such a fool and chastised myself accordingly, angry at my stupidity and frustrated at the prospect of not being able to put things right. It was, in conclusion, tempting to consider my overall position a hopeless one. Everything seemed against me and the options available for effecting an escape appeared practically non-existent. My spirits were low indeed.

I did, however, eventually manage to persuade myself

that I should take full stock of my situation by carrying out a survey of my prison cell and, with that in mind, I climbed gingerly to my feet, one hand pressed against the wall for support. It took me a moment or two to acclimatise to being upright, my head feeling woozy at first as the flow of blood adjusted.

There was still no more light than what little squeezed through between the door and its frame at the top of the stairs, which made it extremely difficult to see. As a result, I found it necessary to cover practically every inch of the floor, bringing myself close to those few objects I did find before I was able to identify them.

Much to my frustration, what little I did discover stored in the cellar was of no real practical benefit to me. In fact, stored was hardly the word to use, since what was there seemed rather to have been abandoned and long since forgotten about, it's days of use judged to be at an end. In one corner there was an old wardrobe, tilted at an alarming angle, due to one of the four corner feet having been knocked off. When I pulled open the door, I found the wardrobe was empty. There was a pair of wicker chairs stacked next to the wardrobe. My nose and fingers suggested these were covered in mould.

My spirits were, for a moment, quite lifted when, on the other side of the room, I stumbled upon an erratically-coiled length of rope, which I immediately considered might afford me some means of setting a trap for my captors. But I cursed my luck when I found the rope so old and weakened by its time in the cellar that strands of it came away in my hands when I inspected it. I doubted it could take even the slightest of weights.

Most disappointing of all, however, was my failure to find anything that might be used as a tool to either pick or break the lock on the door. Of all the things I might have hoped to find, that would have been the most desired.

Puffing out my cheeks and insisting to myself that I not

give up so easily, I turned, finally, to an inspection of the cellar door, climbing the simple wooden stairs with care, lest any of the timbers be rotten. Although I found the lock to be a plain and simple one, of the type normally fitted to such doors, it was quite beyond my abilities to pick it, poorly equipped as I was. Indeed, I doubt I would have been sufficiently skilled even if I had possessed appropriate tools but my efforts with a small length of splintered wood, I pulled away from one of the steps, were hopeless.

It was with regret that I also found both the lock itself and the hinges on the door solid and in good order. Perhaps I might have been able to smash down the door if I had been able to take a good run at it, but that wasn't possible when charging up stairs.

My situation appeared truly bleak and I feared all I could do was wait for the return of Sneijder or perhaps Selkman and make one last effort at fighting for my freedom, not that my prospects seemed bright if my previous encounter with the giant was anything to go by.

With nothing else seeming to be done, I dropped on to the step by the door and sat with my back to the wall, my head in my hands. Anxiety and a sense of hopelessness washed over me. Try as I might, I could think of no way out of my predicament.

*

I remained slumped by the door for nearly an hour, feeling wretched and sorry for myself. I had spent the time reassessing every possibility in the hope of finding something I had not previously spotted, but the options were few and every scheme I laboured to construct was riddled with flaws and impossibilities. I could hardly expect Sneijder to repeat the mistake of sending the housekeeper along with food and drink, although that soon became my most wished for occurrence. I kicked at the wall in frustration and squeezed my hands into fists in an effort to force out some sort of inspiration, but it made no difference.

On two occasions, I heard footsteps approaching along the hallway and tried to peer through the keyhole, but all that was visible was a thin sliver of wall. I called out for help on both occasions, but the first time whoever was passing either didn't hear or chose not to, even when I began hammering on the door with all my might. The second time it was Selkman. He walked over to the door and, in a deep, threatening voice, told me in half a dozen words to be quiet or he'd make me suffer.

It occurred to me that Sneijder had probably taken steps to discourage his patients from coming to my aid. I could imagine with ease that he might well have told them I was dangerous, delusional and to be ignored and avoided at all costs, for their own safety. There was irony in that; the very person who might be able to help those at risk from Sneijder's disgusting activities being accused of having lost his mind.

However, just before six o'clock, I heard footsteps approaching for the third time, once more from the direction of Sneijder's surgery. This time when they reached the door to the cellar, they stopped. All went quiet and I sat upright, tense and listening intently for some sign as to who it was and what might happen next. There was then some shuffling and the key was inserted into the lock.

Every nerve in my body sparked into life and I was on my feet in a moment. I stepped back as far as I could without risk of tumbling down the stairs and set myself, fists clenched, leg muscles tensed and eyes fixed on the door handle, ready to launch myself forward with all my might. This could very well be my last opportunity to secure freedom and, as seemed likely, my life. I had to give things one, final, almighty effort.

The key turned, so slowly I felt I was being tormented, as if they knew I was there, waiting to pounce. I pictured Selkman, standing alongside Sneijder, his feet set like rocks, ready to swat away my assault. My heart was racing and every sound was amplified.

At last, the lock clicked, the handle turned and the door began to ease open. I was ready. Coiled. Determined. I would rather die there and then, trying to escape, than be pushed back down into the cellar, to linger for who knew how long, until Sneijder decided to put me out of my misery. My lips rolled back from my teeth and I was aware my eyes were wide and staring.

I watched the door open, inch-by-inch. A little more, that was all that was needed. Just a little more, so there would be no chance for them to close the door before I hurled myself forward. I twitched in anticipation, my breathing so shallow it hardly took air to my lungs. A little more. Now was the time. I threw myself forward as the door opened wide enough to give me space to clear the threshold.

There was a startled squeal as we fell to the floor in a tangled heap of arms and legs, but no blows were exchanged, nor oaths uttered. Too late, I had seen that the person standing before me was neither Sneijder nor Selkman, nor even the housekeeper, but the unprepared and startled figure of Elizabeth Fitzsimon.

AN UNEXPECTED VISITOR

Disentangling myself, I climbed back on to my feet and helped Miss Fitzsimon do likewise. To her considerable credit, after the initial squeal of horror, she called out no more and I hoped we might have got away without attracting attention to ourselves. As she rubbed at elbows and shoulders and pulled her clothing back into place, I apologised profusely in a whisper of a voice, all the while looking up and down the hallway for any sign of our gaolers. Of those people I might have expected to open the cellar door, Elizabeth Fitzsimon was not among them.

"What are you doing?" I asked rather foolishly, embarrassed at what had happened, but also somewhat confused.

She looked at me as if I was some sort of fool, furrowing her brows, before replying in obvious exasperation, "Rescuing you, of course. What on earth did you think I might be doing?"

"Ah. Yes." I might have blushed if my face was not already red with the tension and effort of my assault. "Silly question. Have you a plan?"

She shook her head. "Just to get you out of that cellar.

Doctor Sneijder said you had been locked down there because you were out of your mind and a danger to all of his patients. We were to leave you well alone."

So I had been right about Sneijder on that score.

"I'm most grateful you chose to ignore him," I said. "I had begun to wonder if I should ever leave that cellar alive."

"That was my thought, also. I couldn't leave you down there, at Sneijder's mercy. I believe the man is capable of the very worst crimes."

I looked along the hallway again, anxious as to the whereabouts of Selkman in particular. "We should leave this place as soon as possible."

She nodded her agreement. "Where will we go?"

I thought for a moment. "Did you see any other houses on your way here from the railway station?"

"None nearby. The last I recall was perhaps two miles away, near a fork in the road."

A fork in the road? I wondered if it could be the same one where the farm labourer and I had been involved in our terrible accident.

I couldn't help but notice my rescuer appeared commendably calm. There was no sign of alarm in her voice nor a look of panic on her face and I suspected that she was rather more composed than I was at that moment. I took a deep breath and tried my best to consider the matter as if I had all the time in the world, anxious not to rush into a hasty and, possibly, soon to be regretted decision.

"Then we shall aim for that fork in the road and see if we can locate the house you saw. It won't be easy if the fog has persisted, but at least we know there is something there to be found."

Again she nodded her agreement. I looked her up and down and realised there was a problem to be addressed before we could proceed. All she had on was her dress and an ordinary pair of shoes. It wouldn't take long once we were outside the house for the cold and damp to start to bite into her flesh and bones.

"We need to find you a coat of some sort and, if we can, stouter footwear."

"The cloakroom is up there," she said, pointing at a door at the end of the hall, across from the surgery.

The risk was obvious. If Sneijder or Selkman should come out of the surgery while we were retrieving coats from the cloakroom, they would be upon us in a moment, certainly before we could effect an escape. But there was no doubt my accomplice was in need of warmer clothing.

"We must be quick about it," I pointed out. "I'm no match for Selkman and if he should see us our chances of escape will be all but gone."

"I understand."

The look on her face was one of determination, which gave me a good degree of confidence there would be no dithering. It was time to get on with things, since every second we lingered put us further at risk.

"Good. Then let us not delay any longer."

We turned as one and walked in silence along the hall. My nerves were once more on edge, but I was also determined. I had been given an opportunity I did not expect and was going to do my utmost to take it. Miss Fitzsimon had put her own safety at risk by choosing to help me and I didn't like to think what retribution Sneijder might visit upon her should we fail in our attempt at escape.

The door to the cloakroom was unlocked. Once inside, we soon each found a coat of suitable size and warmth. Elizabeth was also fortunate enough to find a pair of hiking boots that were a tolerable fit. Once ready, we stood and looked each other in the eye, neither showing any sign of hesitation or loss of nerve, then we turned to make our exit and, we hoped, our escape.

I cautiously opened the cloakroom door just a little,

anxious that we did not blindly tumble out into the arms of Selkman. My lips were dry and I ran the tip of my tongue over them as I listened for any sound of approaching footsteps. There was nothing to be heard, other than the ticking of the clock in the sitting room. It was almost unnervingly quiet.

"The back door?" I whispered the question to Elizabeth, for it had only occurred to me at that point that I did not know where the rear entrance to the house was located.

Elizabeth leaned in close and pointed down the hall to my left, past the sitting room and, beyond that, the dining room and kitchen. "The kitchen," she prompted.

I eased the door open a little more, so that I could see through the crack between the door and the frame, along the hall to my left. It was clear. Filled with anxiety, I pushed the door fully open and stepped out ahead of Elizabeth, who pulled the door shut behind her. It would take us perhaps a single minute to reach the kitchen and the back door. One minute between us and our freedom. I took a deep breath and stepped forward.

At that precise moment, I heard the door to the surgery open. The timing could not possibly have been worse. Thirty seconds sooner and we would still have been in the cloakroom. Thirty seconds later and we would, in all likelihood, have been as far as the dining room and out of sight of anyone exiting the surgery.

Alarmed at the noise, I swung myself around. There, standing stock still, in the doorway to the surgery stood the figure of Sneijder. The startled look on his face made it clear that he was more than a little surprised to see me with Elizabeth coming out of the cloakroom. For the briefest of moments all was silent and static, each of us frozen into inaction by the unexpected turn of events. But that moment evaporated in the blink of an eye and a look of malevolence grew on Sneijder's face.

"Well, what a surprise this is. It seems you have found

yourself an accomplice, Templeman. Such a pity." There was a satisfaction in his voice that was deeply disturbing, threatening even. "Selkman," he barked. "Here. Now."

Again, I had been caught without benefit of anything resembling a weapon. It seemed I was a slow fellow to learn an important lesson. Stepping quickly forward, so as to bring myself alongside Elizabeth, I brought myself up to my full height and raised my fists, ready to fight. My blood was up and I was keen on revenge for what had already happened and what, I felt sure, would follow if Elizabeth and I were not able to make good our escape.

A sickening laugh from Sneijder greeted my challenge before he spoke again. "I admire your persistence, Templeman, but you should know by now that the outcome is a foregone conclusion. You are no match for Selkman."

He glanced to his right as the huge figure of Selkman joined us. There was no grin of pleasure on his face this time; rather a look of utter determination that disturbed me all the more. I hesitated and I'm afraid my eyes betrayed my concern, because in that moment Sneijder lunged at Elizabeth, grabbing her right forearm. She yelled in fright, but, to her credit, had no intention of giving up without a fight of her own. She brought down her right fist on Sneijder's elbow with all the force she could muster and the startled Doctor swore as he let go his grip.

I would have leapt to her help, of course, but by now Selkman had stepped around his master and was closing in on me, his arms raised and his enormous hands closed into fists that looked like sledgehammers. I winced inside and brought my own fists up fully in front of my face in the hope of being able to land a solid blow to his nose, it being one of the most sensitive parts of the human body.

Another scream from my right caused me to take a swift glance sideways. Sneijder had thrown himself at Elizabeth a second time and now had her in a bear hug, lifting her bodily off the ground. She struggled like a devil and hurled insults that would have shocked a dock worker. Fear tore at my insides like some hideous disease and I might have collapsed but for my partner's spirited resistance. If Elizabeth could only keep Sneijder occupied for a minute or two longer, then I might, somehow, be able to fashion a means of bringing down the giant before me. I could, perhaps, be David to his Goliath.

So as to get enough clear space to swing his fists at me, Selkman stepped across the hallway, putting himself between me and the others. But, seeing an opportunity, despite her predicament, Elizabeth planted a lusty kick into the small of Selkman's back, pushing him towards the wall. I seized my chance at once, closing right up to him and crashed two pummelling blows of my own fully into his face. For a second or two, I felt exhilarated by my apparent success, but then my face screwed up in pain as my brain processed the impact of knuckle on jaw. I pulled my hands away, clenching my teeth while trying not to show my agony, which was joined by fear as I saw how little damage my punches had done.

Selkman regained his balance and purpose, that horrible, sickening smirk once more on his face. It seemed as if all my blows had done was to feed him with yet more enthusiasm for the fight. Elizabeth was still struggling, her shouts and oaths ringing in my ears, but there appeared little chance of her breaking free from Sneijder's hold.

I managed to sway away from Selkman's first punch, a straight right jab that would nonetheless have been enough to knock me out, of that I had no doubt, but the second, a short jabbing right, was on me almost before the first had missed and I was not quick enough with my movements to fully evade it. A glancing blow knocked me off balance and I stumbled backwards a step or two, in a state of some shock, I have to admit. But bleak though the situation looked, I couldn't leave things there and determined at once to fight on, righting myself quickly and bringing my fists back up in front of my face, which was by now coated with sweat.

"Run, Alexander. Run."

Elizabeth's shouts took me by surprise. I saw her through the narrow gap between the wall and Selkman's left shoulder. She was no longer struggling and hung like a doll in Sneijder's grip, but there was a sharp look of determination in her fiery eyes, one that told me she had not given up all hope of rescue. The gap through which I glimpsed her disappeared, replaced by the bulk of my opponent, who steadied himself for his next assault. I wasn't sure I could stand a further hit from the heavy artillery that were his fists; it seemed likely that even a second glancing blow might be enough to put me down. I readied myself for a final counter-attack, thinking I might stand a chance of getting in under his guard, seeing how I was so much the smaller man.

"Run, Alexander. Leave me and fetch help. It's our only chance."

Elizabeth's words were insistent rather than desperate, leading me to conclude she had given the situation some thought as she struggled in vain to break free from Sneijder. There was some truth in what she said. My remaining there, to suffer seemingly inevitable defeat at the hands of the Doctor's henchman, would do neither of us any good. On the other hand, if I could escape and bring back help, I would ensure her freedom.

Selkman was big and strong, that was not in doubt, but he appeared not to be as quick as I was. If I could make it out of the house and into the open countryside there seemed every chance of achieving my freedom. I certainly had little left to lose from making the effort.

"I will be back, you can be sure of that," I yelled to Elizabeth, even as I began to turn.

Something brushed the back of my hair and I heard

Selkman's fist slam into the wall. It was a very near miss indeed. No longer hesitating, I burst into a sprint, working my legs for all they were worth as I raced for the sitting room. A commotion erupted behind me, but I forced myself to ignore it and focused on my goal. I flew through the sitting room and on into the dining room, pulling chairs to the floor behind me as I raced by them, in the hope they would delay my pursuer.

I paused only as I reached the door to the kitchen, when I looked sharply to my left to see how great was my lead. As I did so, Selkman, in attempting to leap one of the chairs that had been knocked to the ground, caught a foot and fell to the in such a violent crash that the building seemed to shudder. I smiled, happy at my fortune, took a deep breath and pushed open the door before me. Rushing across the small, uncluttered kitchen, I grabbed hold of the handle to the outside door and, for a moment, felt terrified that it might be locked. But the handle turned without resistance and, as I swung open the last obstacle to my containment, there was still no sign of Selkman. Thick, smothering fog greeted me like an old and welcome friend. I launched myself into it with sheer delight. My lungs filled with with cold air as I ran, causing them to burn at the sudden change in temperature, but I cared not a fig and rushed onwards. The fog had been the reason for my arrival at the house and for my remaining there so long, but now it seemed its part in events had changed and it was to be my saviour.

A CHANGE OF HEART

I had the good fortune to find myself running across a scruffy lawn which, although slippery as the result of being so damp, was at least flat and unobstructed. Across it I fled, until stumbled into a border of dormant shrubs. I was only just able to slow my advance in time to avoid tearing myself to pieces on the sharp branches that jutted out in all directions. Breathing heavily, I looked back over my shoulder. There was no sign of Selkman. Things were, for once, going in my favour.

With my heart beating like a drum from the exhilaration of the chase, I tried to think through my next move; one which I hoped would take me to the road that ran past the house and do so without my stumbling into my pursuer. I couldn't be certain where the road lay in relation to my position since I had arrived at the house from the opposite direction and in a state of some confusion. I briefly considered making my way round to the other side of the building, but the risk of being discovered seemed too great. It was clear that, in respect of his knowledge of the land, Selkman had a considerable advantage over me and was, no doubt, at that very moment plotting his own next move.

It occurred to me that the next part of this fearful game we were engaged in would be rather like chess, as we attempted to outwit each other in the semi-blindness of the ever present fog. Seeing my situation in such terms brought a broad smile to my face, for I felt confident I possessed the sharper brain of the two of us. On the other hand, should Sneijder become involved, the situation would be very different indeed.

Then, barely visible through the fog, I saw a silhouette of a figure emerge into the garden from the kitchen. There could be no doubt who it was, since Selkman was by far the largest fellow in the house. I dropped slowly to my haunches, watching all the time, nerves beginning once more to pick at my confidence. But I needn't have worried, for Selkman stole silently around to the front of the house, no doubt thinking I would make a bid to retrace my tracks in the hope of finding one of the few cottages or farms I had passed in the farm cart.

With Selkman gone from the scene, I began to pick my way through the border until I came to what appeared to be a small copse of mixed trees, some pine, some birch and others I couldn't name. I should have pushed on, I knew very well, but, looking back once more at the house, almost vanished into the fog, I felt a pang of guilt and a sense that I was running away when I should have been standing my ground. There was no need for such thoughts, of course, since Elizabeth had made her wishes very clear, but, all the same, I could not push them from my mind. So, in a state of some confusion, I entered the edge of the copse and dropped on to my heels in the lee of a rough-barked pine, the scent of which was so clear and persistent that even the damp air of the fog could not stop it reaching my nostrils.

What, I wondered, was I to do? My original aim seemed a sound one. Make good my escape, so narrowly won, then find assistance and return to rescue Elizabeth and her fellow patients. It should have been a straightforward matter for me to press on. Lord knows, I had no idea how long it would take me to find some lonely cottage or hillside farm. Lingering there in the trees was only going to delay the matter.

But, still I could not bring myself to move. Guilt and fear gnawed away at me like two hungry fellows who had alighted on a splendid meal. The guilt, of course, was the thought that I was running away like a veritable coward, too afraid to face the challenge and risk injury or more. There was some truth in that, after all, for the prospect of having my neck broken by the hands of Selkman was a real one and no man wants to give up his life so young, especially when there seemed so little hope of defeating my opponents. All the same, I would have put my life on the line if there was not the very real possibility of some other more likely means of salvation.

No, it was not guilt but rather fear that made me hesitate when I seemed on the brink of victory. Even if I did manage to avoid getting lost on the hills and found some sort of assistance, what might we find upon our return? Could Sneijder really risk a brazen attempt at bluffing his way out of a sticky situation? Should he be challenged, he would insist, no doubt, that, as a result of my concussion, I had been suffering from wild delusions that caused me to imagine all manner of outrages. And as for his patients, including Elizabeth, he could merely point out that each one of them was there for the very reason they needed his specialist attention to help them recover from mental and emotional illness.

Perhaps, under other circumstances, such a defence might prove enough to save the Doctor, but I was as certain as could be that Elizabeth would prove to be a firm and persistent opponent of the Doctor and that in turn might well turn the situation against him.

And there was the real problem. If Sneijder should

either not have the nerve to bluff his way through the situation or came to the conclusion that any such attempt would more than likely result in failure, then his only option, it appeared to me, would be to put an end to those who might prove his guilt. For the time being, I was at no risk of harm, but Elizabeth was in a wholly desperate situation, her safety anything but assured.

That was the real cause of my hesitation. A growing sense of dread that, if I left there and then, by the time I returned it would be to find Elizabeth brutally murdered. It wasn't beyond the bounds of possibility that Sneijder might try to dress it up as some terrible accident, thereby leaving no one to collaborate my story, for I felt certain the other three patients I had encountered were not up to doing any such thing.

I rolled my right fist in the palm of my left hand and knew my mind was made up. I was not going any further. No, I was determined to take on and defeat my opponents and thereby deprive them of the chance to silence Elizabeth for ever. Now all I needed to do was work out some scheme by which I could give myself a half-decent chance of success.

A PLAN OF ACTION

Taking care to retain the cover afforded by the trees and the shrubbery, as well as keeping myself crouched low, I made my way in an awkward gait along the outer edge of the garden until I came to a spot where a denser clump of planting and the tall, weather-beaten stump of a felled tree gave me a good place to hide. From there I had a decent, if fog restricted, view of both the front and rear doors. While I waited for Selkman to return, for I wanted him inside the house, I began to turn over several possibilities for some feasible scheme that would give me the upper hand in the coming struggle.

It was close on fifteen minutes later that I heard the soft tread of footsteps coming up the drive to my right; a long stride that warned me of Selkman's approach. It was him I saw emerge through the fog close to the house. Although I was confident I could not be seen, instinct still caused me to crouch lower and deeper into my cover, as if I feared just the scent of me would alert him to my presence. For one breath-stopping moment I thought he had heard me and was intent on carrying out a search, for, just short of the front door, he stopped and turned, peering through those harsh, searching eyes of his for some sign of his quarry. But, after a moment, he turned back and entered the house through the front door, shutting it with barely a sound, and I breathed freely once more.

It occurred to me next that if I was to stand any chance of coming up with a tolerable plan then I needed to better acquaint myself with the terrain, so I set off to carry out a reconnaissance of the land and several outbuildings dotted around the property. Taking care not to tread like the amateur I was on some branch or twig that might snap with a crack loud enough to risk exposing me, I stole yard by yard across the lawn outside the kitchen, then around the back of the house. Here I found a well-equipped workshop, unlocked, with tools of all kinds, many that would make a fine choice for a weapon, and all the usual mass of timber, metal and sundry other items that may prove themselves of use. It was the very best discovery I could have hoped for and I moved on to further explorations with my confidence well restored.

Alongside the workshop was a large, well-stocked timber-framed log store, the contents of which appeared to have been recently sawn and split. Leaning against one of the inner panels was a huge axe, the blade of which was well-maintained and without doubt capable of splitting a man's head wide open. I picked it up and felt its considerable weight in my hands, before trying a swing or two, to see how I might fare with it in a fight, But, despite its obvious attractions, I decided I had not the build or the strength in my arms and shoulders to use it effectively and concluded I would be too slow and cumbersome to gain an advantage if I did not hit home cleanly with my first attempt. With some reluctance, I placed it back where I found it.

After moving to the far edge of the lawn running along the back of the house, I pressed on across the damp grass, the water now beginning to seep into my leather shoes, leaving my feet wet and my socks clinging. Moisture was also by now building up on my face and I had to wipe it away several times to stop it from dripping into my eyes.

There was but one more outbuilding to explore, a large timber structure set back from the house on the far edge of the property. It was in poor repair, ivy covering much of the sides and a large part of the roof, which itself was holed in several places. The double doors at the front were padlocked and when I managed to wipe away enough dirt from the single window on the near side, to peer in, it appeared the place was empty, save for a few pieces of timber scattered on the floor.

If I had walked forward from this structure, I would have passed along the side of the house with Sneijder's surgery and arrived at the top of the driveway. But there was nothing to be gained from such a risky venture, since there appeared to be nothing of interest there. Instead, I returned to the workshop, by far the most useful of my discoveries, to decide on my next course of action.

Sitting there in the cold and poorly lit interior of the workshop, I was reminded of those days in my youth when I had used my father's well-equipped workshop as a base of operations from which I would launch sorties against my cousins, who were holed up in the stables, as we played out scenes from exciting battles fought across the Empire. It had, of course, been nothing more than a game then, but it was deadly serious now; quite literally a matter of life and death.

Turning over ideas in my head as to how to get the upper hand with Selkman, I was reminded how frequently it had been the case in those games of my youth that the winner of an engagement would be the party who gained a surprise advantage. Rarely did the startled combatant have an opportunity to regroup and launch an effective counter-attack. That, I decided, was to be my tactic now. But how to achieve sufficient surprise?

I had faced the giant twice now, on both occasions in confined space where my greater speed and agility was of little, if any, advantage, and Selkman had come out on top both times. Despite managing to escape him the second time, there was no hiding the fact he had been getting the better of things. If it did not suit me to face him inside the house, perhaps I would fare better outside, preferably in the open where there were no impediments to my movement and where Selkman might appear something of a lumbering giant, easily hit by a man of fleeter foot.

I looked around me again, taking a keener eye to those tools I had at my disposal. As I did so, a thought came to me that caused me to hesitate and re-assess my situation. Whilst I was clear on my objective of freeing Elizabeth from Sneijder's clutches, one thing I had not so far debated was just how far I was prepared to go to make this happen and to take care of my own safety. Sneijder had made it clear during my time in the cellar that he considered my life forfeit. Since I was about to expose myself to the risk of being recaptured and then murdered, was I prepared to end another person's life if it came down to that? It was a terrible action to contemplate; one no ordinary man, outside the theatre of war, has normally to consider. I struggled with myself as I considered the prospect, but there was no getting away from the fact that such an action may turn out to be necessary and I decided to prepare myself accordingly.

There were several vicious-looking knives, any one of which was surely sufficient to puncture a man with a deep and potentially fatal wound. I picked up one of them, a bone-handled affair with a blade some seven or eight inches long, and made several jabbing and cutting movements at some imaginary opponent. It was tempting to make it my choice, but it would mean getting in exceedingly close to Selkman and I feared giving him a chance to reach me with those enormous, powerful hands. I reached the same conclusion when considering a half-dozen hand hammers, most of which I could easily swing in a controlled manner with just the one hand, but that too would mean closing right up on Selkman.

As I began to think that perhaps I would have to take a chance with a knife, I uncovered a long-handled hammer with a heavy wooden head. What it might be used for I did not know, but when I weighed it in my hands it felt solid enough to cause a man some damage, yet not so heavy or sizeable that I might find myself struggling to control it. What was more, I judged it had a reach of a little under three feet; sufficient to keep me beyond Selkman's immediate grasp. That, I decided, would be my weapon and I stood it, along with a small pocket knife as a fall back, next to the door.

There was a small, dust-coated window in the workshop and I took a moment to peer out towards the house. I had a partial view of both the dining room and the sitting room. The curtains remained open in every window, but there was no sign of movement inside either room, whilst the kitchen was on the other side of the house, out of my view. I shivered, the cold beginning to leach in through my clothes. It occurred to me that in another hour, perhaps one hour and a half, the light would start to fade and darkness would see the temperature fall a great deal. Whatever I was going to do, I needed to move forward with soon.

How then to encourage Selkman to leave the confines of the house? I needed some means of enticing him out into the open, something that he would not be able to resist and, if possible, that would also distract him from seeing my approach. What I wanted was the perfect ambush, one that would afford him no opportunity of fighting back.

Smoke began to climb away reluctantly from one of the chimneys, barely creeping up through the heavy damp fog. It made me feel all the colder, crouching there in the unheated workshop as my bones began to feel the chill. It was then that the idea came to me, a veritable flash of inspiration. Fire would force Selkman from the house. If I was to place a good number of dry timbers up against a suitable point of the house and ensure there was properly combustible kindling underneath them, all I had to do was set it alight, retreat to my hideaway and wait. Once the fire properly took hold, someone in the house would be sure to notice the flames or smoke and out would come the one man most likely to be sent to deal with it. Then, like a big cat on the Savannah, I could spring from my cover and put Selkman down with a single, heaving blow of my hammer.

It seemed a sensible enough plan, I thought, despite my attempts at finding weaknesses in it, and was certainly one that would offer the advantage I sought. I therefore collected together from the stores inside the workshop a fine assortment of timber, some of which was of rather good quality and a shame to set to flame, but there was no room for sentimentality. For kindling, I filled my pockets with several rags and then a small bucket with numerous wooden off-cuts.

Surveying the house again, I determined the best place to position my bonfire would be under the sitting room window. It was the room most likely to be used at such a time and there was a possibility that the fire might also be seen from either the hallway or the dining room. It also meant I would have perhaps ten yards of open ground to cover in my approach to Selkman, a distance I was confident I could complete quickly enough to avoid detection before striking with my hammer.

My excitement grew as the prospect of implementing my plan came closer and I worked happily and quickly to build my fire, making several trips between the workshop and the house, crouched low and my arms filled with timbers. All the while the house remained silent and apparently deserted.

The final trip completed and the kindling set in place, I smiled to myself, pleased with my handiwork and eager to strike the match that would ignite the whole thing into raging flames and billowing smoke. Then, in the blink of an eye, my heart sank and my whole body wilted. What a fool. A match. I needed a match to light the fire and yet I had none. I cursed myself for making such a mistake. Creeping back to the workshop, I searched in vain for a box of matches, or anything else that might generate a spark. Still angry with myself, I considered my options. The kitchen. There was sure to be a box of matches in the kitchen, if nowhere else in the house.

But entering the house, even for a brief moment, was not a prospect I relished. If my luck should run out and Selkman found me there, my plans for surprise and ambush would be gone in an instant. Such a fool! I cursed myself again. But there was no getting away from it, I had no choice but to enter the kitchen in search of matches.

Stealing around the end of the house, I positioned myself behind a section of shrubbery where I had a tolerable view of the kitchen window and observed the place for a minute or so, anxious not to stumble in when the housekeeper was there. Confident the place was empty, I sprinted across the lawn, my nerves jangling and my body tense, opened the door and stepped inside, ready for the worst to happen. Nothing greeted me but silence and the enticing, spicy smell of a fruit cake baking in the oven.

Almost at once I found a large box of matches on a shelf by the oven, which I slipped into a jacket pocket. There was also there a plate covered over with a cloth. I felt suddenly hungry, no doubt the smell of the cake doing its worst, and when I lifted the towel I found a plate piled high with warm ginger biscuits. I helped myself to a handful, then turned and fled from the room as the sound of voices arose in the adjoining dining room.

NO SMOKE WITHOUT FIRE

As the door to the kitchen closed with a firm click, I dropped low at once and crept away, pressed tight up to the side of the house, my jacket brushing the brickwork. My heart was thumping and I kept glancing over my shoulder towards the kitchen door, certain that Selkman or Sneijder would step through and find me. When I at last rounded the corner of the building and moved out of immediate sight of the kitchen door, I stopped, with my back pressed hard against the wall, and closed my eyes. Relief washed over me in tingling waves; the risk had paid off and my ability to spring a surprise remained intact.

Having taken several deep breaths and regained some composure, I turned once more to the matter of igniting the fire and, remaining low, to avoid being seen through the dining room windows, I continued along the back of the house until I reached my stack of timbers. With the box of matches in my pocket, everything now seemed set for me to put my plan into action.

But at that moment, the same voices I heard from the kitchen, one a man and the other a woman, appeared to approach the dining room windows, fragments of a conversation growing louder by the second. I cursed my bad fortune at this late stage in proceedings, but had no choice other than to keep my head down and the matches in my pocket, away from the damp of the fog.

What with the cold and damp, that had by now made its way into every part of my clothing and attached itself with much persistence to my skin, and the repeated stressing of my nerves, I began to feel as though if things were not over soon, then I may not last the course. That surge of enthusiasm and energy that had filled me so happily when I settled on my scheme was beginning to wane.

It wasn't possible for me to make out who was talking in the dining room, the walls and the window deadening the nuance of their voices most effectively, but I was certain they were not far from me. Although my legs had begun to suffer in their squashed and unnatural position, I dare not shift my weight, for fear of giving myself away. I was, therefore, forced to wait things out until, at last, those voices began to move away and, finally, to vanish from my hearing altogether.

As a sensible precaution, I waited another minute or two, straightened out my legs to give them some relief, then edged along to the nearest window and, with great caution, peered inside to ascertain whether or not the coast was clear. I puffed out my cheeks, relieved to see the room empty and no sign that anyone was planning to return.

With immediate danger gone, it was essential that I press on with setting my fire without further delay. It simply wasn't possible that my luck would hold forever. I moved back to my pile of timbers, where I crouched low, so as to be close to the kindling, then struck up a match. The screwed-up paper that sat at the very bottom of the pile caught almost at once, bright, eager flames leapt high. I smiled in satisfaction at the spectacle. But I could not be complacent, so remained where I was for several minutes, until I was entirely happy that the wood shavings had been taken by the flames and they, in turn, were licking promisingly at the larger timbers, which I could see begin to blacken and smoulder.

My fire looking well set, I checked once more through the dining room window that I would not be seen, then ran the short distance to the workshop, into which I tumbled, pulling the door closed behind me. The tiredness and worry I had felt hiding outside the dining room soon left me entirely and I found myself filled with energy and eagerness once more.

Flames were soon licking high up the wall of the house, smoke tapering off into the foggy sky, while the smell of it drifted across to where I hid, waiting for my opponent to show his face. The anticipation had me restless, unable to stand still and my fingers constantly exercised themselves in readiness for what was to follow.

After five minutes of waiting in vain, I began to grow a little restless. After six, I was somewhat concerned the house would begin to burn. Of Selkman, or anyone else, there had been no sign. No alarmed face at the window, horrified by what they could see. No screams of panic from within. And most definitely no one running towards the flames from the kitchen with the intention of putting out the now fiercely burning fire. Indeed, so strong was the fire by this stage that I could feel the heat upon my face, which did at least fend off some of the cold that had molested me since I had left the warmth of the house.

Finally, as I began to wonder if anyone inside the house would notice the danger, I saw the huge, hulking figure of Selkman peer out of the dining room window. From where I was, he looked little more than a shadow, lit up here and there by the burning light that danced across the crackling timbers. He saw the fire at once, though he would have been hard pushed to miss it, and turned on his heels without a moment's hesitation. A thrill ran through me as I reached out a hand to take hold of the wooden hammer.

Finally, my moment was almost with me. If I could but take down this huge, powerful man then my way would be clear, for I could not see the housekeeper or even Sneijder being able to get the better of me.

I was a little taken aback by the sight of Selkman as he raced round the corner of the house, for he moved somewhat faster than I had given him credit for and looked more certain on his feet than most big men do. He did not hesitate with assessments and appraisals as he reached the burning timbers, but set about them right away, kicking at the base of the bonfire with his feet, trying to dislodge things as best he could and steer them away from the building.

Happily for me, he was a man engrossed in his work entirely. Picking up the wooden hammer and taking a deep breath to better steel myself, I pushed open the workshop door and, without a pause or second thought, walked straight across the ground so as to bring myself up directly behind him. My heart rate and breathing quickened as I closed on him, bringing the hammer up level with my head.

Selkman took a considerable swing at one of the largest timbers with his foot and, as he did so, his body turned a fraction to his left. This movement appeared to provide him with a glimpse of me, for he paused and started to turn his head further in my direction. If I had been a yard or two further away, I may have been in a good degree of trouble and fearing for the worst, but I was almost on top of him and, lifting the hammer higher still, I brought it down on his unnaturally large skull with very nearly as much force as I could manage. I only held back at all because, at the last moment, some little part of me did not want to snuff out the man's life, despite the danger he presented to me if I did not put him down.

There was a terrible, violent thump, the impact of which rippled up the handle of the hammer and on up my arms, before the weapon fell away to one side. The sound of solid timber on skull was an odd, rather dull thud, that was nothing like they describe it in the more sensational of adventure stories. A short, deep sigh escaped Selkman's open mouth, then, after a momentary pause, he slumped to the ground as if every one of his bones had been turned to dust. He lay there in an unnatural distortion of a sleeping man, his arms folded under his body.

My blood was up and I stood there, wide-eyed and excited, my hands gripping the handle of the hammer so tightly that the devil himself would not have been able to prise it from them. I am ashamed to admit now that a part of me wanted Selkman to rise up and threaten to set about me, so that I could let him have a second blow and perhaps then a third. Those animal instincts that are buried deep inside us all had taken control of me, of that there was no doubt. It was a most disturbing sensation, both unexpected and unsettling in its nature.

It was fortunate for me that, as I stood there looking down over the prostrate figure of my opponent, my breathing began to settle, my heart rate returned to something more normal and, little by little, I began to take back control of myself. Keeping a grip on the hammer with one hand, I bent down next to Selkman and sought out a pulse. It reminded me of my inadequate attempts to do just that very thing with the farm labourer after the cart had crashed, but on this occasion there was a sense of relief in me when I found a solid enough pulse on the side of Selkman's neck. He was very much out of the game but still alive, for which I gave thanks to the Heavens.

With Selkman, the only one of my three adversaries that I truly feared, now disposed of, I felt a calmness begin to wash over me. An odd sensation, given the situation I was in at that time, but I welcomed it all the same, for I believed it gave me back my senses and allowed me to make rational decisions again, not ones driven by base, animal instincts.

I stood there for a moment in the silence, interrupted only by the sparking and crackling of what remained of the fire, and wondered what I was to do next. The odd thing was, I hadn't given my next step a single thought when planning my little ambush on Selkman, which now seemed a somewhat peculiar shortcoming. It was a plan only half devised. But then, as I found myself staring intently into a cluster of flames, a funny thought came to me. It was such a simple and amusing idea that I really couldn't resist it.

Not wanting to run the risk of the house catching fire, I used the hammer to knock away from the wall the remaining burning timbers, which began, almost at once, to fizzle and die on the wet, cold ground. When that job was completed, I retrieved a length of strong rope from the workshop and proceeded to tie up Selkman in a manner I hoped would hold him secure, should he regain his senses before I was done with his confederates.

The risk of a major fire averted and Selkman secured, I dusted off my sooty clothes and straightened them up, then wiped the worst of the dirt and stains from my hands on the damp grass. All I had to do now was march around to the front of the house and pull vigorously on the doorbell, which is precisely what I did. I suppose it must have been something of a surprise to those inside to hear the doorbell ring, but, whether it was or not, the door was soon opened.

THE RETURN OF A STRANGER

No doubt I made a quite remarkable sight, standing there rather a mess, grasping a large wooden hammer, when it must have been accepted by Sneijder and his confederates that I had fled far away into the fog. That probably accounted somewhat for the rather satisfying look of open-mouthed astonishment that appeared on Sneijder's face as soon as he set eyes on me, standing on the threshold to his den of evil. He seemed rooted to the spot, as if frozen by shock. I could have danced a merry jig of celebration, so pleased was I with the impact I made.

However, there was no time for gloating and complacency, for there was still work to be done and I had no desire to hand the initiative back to Sneijder when it belonged, as it did then, entirely to me.

"Quite a pleasant evening, wouldn't you say, Sneijder? Things seem to have turned out rather splendidly, after all."

Giving him no chance to reply, I took the hammer in both hands, brought it up swiftly in front of me, then pushed it with some force into the Doctor's chest. He stumbled backwards into the hallway, only just able to keep himself upright, his arms waving wildly at his sides. I stepped over the threshold, pushed the Doctor a little further back, so as to give myself space to enter the hallway, and closed the door behind me with the heel of one foot. I smiled at Sneijder; although some might say it was more of smirk.

"Not expecting me back so soon, eh?"

Sneijder looked alarmed, as well he might, his face rather pale and his eyes flicking down at the hammer, still tightly in my grasp, then back up at me, no doubt wondering what I had in mind. It may not have been the gentlemanly thing to do to make sport of him, but I struggled with myself not to so do as I recalled the enthusiasm with which he had locked me in the cellar and threatened to put a permanent end to my meddling in his affairs.

"Not to worry, I don't expect to be staying long. In matter of fact, I aim to conclude my business here very promptly."

I shifted the hammer up and down three or four times in my hands, as if I might be weighing it up, ready to strike a blow. Sneijder took half a step further back, glancing again at the hammer.

"You won't get away with this, Templeman," he replied, the wobble in his voice betraying his nervousness.

"Won't I? And who will stop me?"

I knew full well what was on his mind by way of salvation and the hopelessness of such a thought, but I couldn't help continuing the game a little longer.

"Selkman," shouted the Doctor, recovering his voice and straightening his posture a little. "Selkman, come to the hallway at once."

I smiled again and tilted my head to one side, as if trying to pick out the sound of an approaching man, his running feet heavy on the carpets. Of course, there was no such sound.

"You appear to have been abandoned," I added innocently. "Whatever could have happened to the charming Selkman?" Again I weighed the hammer in my hands, to emphasise my point.

"Selkman," he yelled again, though this time there was more hope than expectation in his voice.

"Selkman won't be running along to help you," I stated in a matter-of-fact manner. "I've put your giant out of action. You are on your own now, Sneijder."

Alarm blossomed on Sneijder's face, his eyes wide. He looked hard to his right, along the hallway, then back at me as he stepped still further away. I closed the gap to its original distance, happy now that I had enjoyed my little bit of fun and an element of revenge. My position of strength was now clearly established in Sneijder's mind and it was time to bring matters to a conclusion, starting with the whereabouts of Elizabeth.

"Now, tell me where you've locked up Miss Fitzsimon," I demanded, jabbing the head of the hammer towards Sneijder's midriff.

"She's in her room," he stammered.

It was quite the transformation that had come over Sneijder, his pasty face filled with fear and all the self-assurance and authority he had possessed before gone in a moment. I suppose some men are like that; bullies, full of themselves when things are wholly in their favour, then a shallow, empty vessel when the world takes a turn against them. But I kept my guard up all the same, anxious not to be caught out by any ruse on the part of my opponent, a man I felt it best not to trust so much as an inch.

"Do you have the keys to the room?" I demanded.

"They are on my desk." He looked towards his surgery.

I flicked the hammer in the direction of the surgery to direct him there and he did as he was bid, with me following two yards behind, confident now that I would be able to bring things to a successful conclusion. That made it all the more of a shock when I heard an ugly, thick-accented command thrown at me from the sitting room doorway.

"Stop where you are, sonny boy, or I'll shoot you dead."

They do say that a man is at his most vulnerable when he is overly-confident and it seemed I was guilty of that very crime, for I had grossly under-estimated the threat from the housekeeper. Indeed, I had not considered her any threat at all to my well thought out plan. But as I stopped and turned around, I found myself staring down the length of the hallway at the figure of an evil-looking woman hunched over a revolver which she held in a way that suggested she had some familiarity with the thing. It was, of course, pointing directly at me.

There was now a roar of delight from behind me as Sneijder realised the tables had turned again. I was caught in a pincer movement, nowhere to go but up the stairs, if I could make it without being shot down. It was a strange sensation, standing there in mortal danger and with little chance of escape, as my mind raced through a cold, careful calculation of my chances of success under several scenarios in little more than a second or two. I felt my senses heighten and my body tense for action, but there was, oddly, no overwhelming sensation of fear of imminent death, which I might have expected under the circumstances.

I do not even remember consciously kicking my body into action when my mind was made up, for it all seemed to happen in some peculiar world of which I was more a spectator than an active participant, though of course, I was very much involved indeed.

Not wishing to allow Sneijder the opportunity to disarm me, I acted swiftly and swung the hammer at him. Just as I intended, the blow caught him solidly on the side of the knee, which brought from his mouth a scream of anguished pain. In the very moment of doing so, my legs began to drive me forward and I picked up speed faster than I thought possible as I hurtled down the hallway, my target as clear to her as it was to me.

I don't recall the sound of the gun firing, but I do remember the flash from the muzzle, bright as the sun for the briefest of moments. I was doing my level best to dart first left, then right, so as to make myself a more difficult target, but at such close range I was heavily relying on the housekeeper not being the best of shots. I don't recall whether I saw the flash from the gun or felt the pain in my right thigh first, but I don't suppose it matters a great deal. The bullet ripped through the material of my trousers and tore a line across the skin underneath. The burning sensation that flared up in my leg was instant and considerable and, for a brief moment, I lost a little of my momentum. But I couldn't stop, for to do so would be fatal, and, breathing heavily now, blood rushing through my veins as fast as my heart could pump it, I ran on.

It would have been an interesting question to debate, as to whether it was the housekeeper or I who was the more surprised that I reached her before she could aim a second shot at me. The weapon did fire again, but it happened at the precise moment I crashed into the woman and the bullet buried itself safely in the ceiling of the hallway as the two of us went crashing and sprawling across the sitting room floor.

The force of the impact was so great that it took me a moment, lying there on the carpet, to regain my senses. My right shoulder ached terribly and for a moment I feared I might have dislocated it, but I managed to roll it a little, which confirmed it was nothing more than sore. The pain was pretty bad as I climbed back on to my feet, breathing deeply and blinking my eyes so as to refocus them.

A groan, then a foul-mouthed complaint, arose from behind the sofa opposite me. I quickly looked about me, hoping to spot the revolver, but there was no sign of it, which had me on edge at once, since there was now every possibility the housekeeper still had it in her possession. As a woman's hand appeared on the back of the sofa, I was, I have to admit, taken somewhat by a sense of panic, fearful in the extreme that the woman would bring the revolver over the top of the sofa and aim it squarely at my person. It was a silly thing to do and would have been of no real aid in even the least threatening of situations, but I grabbed hold of the only thing within my reach: a book on Scottish birdlife that lay on top of a small side table to my left.

To my utter astonishment, the damned woman was up on her feet like a shot, despite the collision she had suffered, her face wild with fury and hurling the most venomous insults at me. Even before I could make a move towards her, the housekeeper's right arm arced up over her shoulder and a lump of firewood hurtled towards my head. Ducking at the last moment, so the wood did no more than brush my hair, I swooped down into a crouch, then launched myself towards the sofa and the housekeeper, intending to knock her back to the ground.

But she was quick enough to side-step my assault and, as I knocked over the sofa and tumbled away across the floor, she grabbed hold of a wooden chair and came at me with it, her eyes unnaturally large and filled with hatred, while her hair had turned into some astonishing tangle that even the most untidy of birds would refuse to nest in. My shoulder continued to hamper my movements, but I tried not to let that show for fear it would encourage the woman's thoughts of victory, and we were by now both breathing heavily from our exertions.

A bead of sweat began to trickle down the side of my face and I would have liked to wipe it away, but I kept my hands raised up in front of me, ready to grab hold of one of the chair's legs if the housekeeper should make a mistake and let me get close enough. But she kept a distance, prodding and jabbing the chair legs at me, trying her best to tease a false move out of me, so she could take advantage and strike me down. It was a tense affair and I don't mind saying that I feared the worst.

Then, quite out of the blue, from somewhere towards the Doctor's surgery, came the sound of glass breaking. It was only a fleeting distraction, but it was enough to take away the housekeeper's attention, as her eyes darted towards the source of the noise. Seizing my opportunity, I lunged forward, intending to pull away the chair she held, but she was obscenely powerful for a woman and held her grip, wailing and screaming her curses all the time. We struggled for supremacy and the chair jolted this way then that, several times over, until I realised I had another option. As the chair shifted back towards the housekeeper, I put all my weight behind it and knocked her a second time to the floor.

As the woman fell on her back, the chair buried itself in my chest, lifting my feet from the ground before tipping me away to the right, where I came crashing down on the far end of the sofa. My word, my ribs took a pounding and I lay there a moment or two gasping for breath as the pain seemed to fill my whole chest. Still struggling to breathe as stabs of pain burned up my left flank, I staggered to my feet, bent over and unsteady, my head giddy.

"Ah, I've got yeah now," I heard the woman cackle, the delight clear in her voice.

Lifting my head, then slowly straightening my back while doing my best to ignore the pain in my chest, I looked at the woman, now standing behind the armchair nearest the door. In her hands she held the revolver again and it was, of course, pointed at me. I had not the energy or speed of movement left to make another dash at her and it seemed all I could do was prepare myself as best I could for the inevitable.

"You be going to meet yer maker now," she spat.

I started on an effort to compose myself, thinking I could at least depart the world with my self-respect intact and avoid giving the housekeeper the pleasure of hearing me plead for mercy, for she clearly believed this was not a time to take prisoners. She raised the revolver a little further, to sharpen her aim. I saw her right index finger caress the trigger and I thought to pray, when, in a blur of action, something rushed at her from the hallway and a length of timber came crashing down on her head. As the housekeeper's eyes glazed over and closed, the gun slipped from her grasp, before she slumped to the floor in a crumpled heap.

Now the housekeeper was no longer on her feet to obstruct the view, I found myself looking into the startled, though undeniably determined, eyes of Elizabeth Fitzsimon, still holding a length of timber in her hands. We said nothing, merely stared at each other for a short while until I began to laugh, despite the pain it brought to my chest; a release, no doubt, for the appalling tension I had experienced as death had seemed certain to strike me down.

Elizabeth let the timber fall to the ground, then smiled at me as I dropped on to the nearest sofa and let my head rest against its back. If I had not been laughing, it is entirely possible I would instead have cried, such was my relief.

THE LOCK BREAKER CONFESSES

I was sitting at a small, battered wooden table in the kitchen, opposite Elizabeth Fitzsimon, nursing a very welcome cup of hot, strong tea and gorging myself on a huge slab of obscenely thickly buttered bread, from which little bits of strawberry jam fell on to the table-top every now and then. Elizabeth sipped at her own cup of tea, silent, watching as I ate my first meal of any note since the morning. It was only then that I noticed her eyes were the deepest blue, as befitted a woman with such beautiful blonde hair. Those eyes were filled with happiness for the first time since I had met Elizabeth; before then, they had always been filled with dread and apprehension.

A little earlier, as she had tended to my various injuries, she had told me that she had not been at dinner on my first evening in the house because Sneijder had insisted she remain in her room for fear I might be a sinister sort of chap, intent on causing mischief. The housekeeper had taken dinner up to her on a tray and she ate alone, deeply unhappy and anxious to make my acquaintance, especially if it should appear I might be someone in whom she could safely confide her concerns.

Sneijder had not been able to hide from the patients the fact that someone new had arrived, unexpectedly; not when there had been such a commotion after Selkman scooped me up off the driveway and carried me inside, initially into the Doctor's surgery. Indeed, James Scurry had seen me in Selkman's arms, only briefly, but it was enough for Sneijder to have no chance of denying my arrival.

It seemed likely that Sneijder had been determined for her not to talk to me because he felt she was not yet sufficiently under his spell, unlike Camilla Downing, who, even now, remained somewhat in a daze. As a result, when Elizabeth encountered me in the sitting room, she had to make a snap judgement as to my character, though she readily admitted she knew she was taking something of a chance in speaking to me the way she did; I could, after all, have been allied to Sneijder and his confederates in some way. She had been mightily relieved when it became clear I was not at all in league with them.

My initial attempt at escape, when I gave her the chance to go with me, had at first filled Elizabeth with a degree of hope she had not experienced since her first day in Sneijder's hands. Our capture only made her outrage and determination all the greater and when she had established that I had been locked in the cellar, denounced as a mad man and a threat to everyone else in the house, she knew at once she must do everything in her power to set me free.

I must admit, I laughed heartily when she informed me that she was something of an expert at picking a lock, something she had learned from a fellow pupil at boarding school in Surrey. By all accounts, the lock on her room was weakened from lack of maintenance and she was able to free herself with a minimum of effort. At this point, I used the whiskey Elizabeth poured for me to toast that schoolfriend of hers, for without that unofficial addition to the school curriculum, I might very well have rotted in that horrible, cold cellar.

After Elizabeth had patched me up so that I was fit to move around again, albeit with some pain in my ribs and my right leg, we together dragged then carried the unconscious housekeeper down into that same cellar and locked the door with great care. I may smile now, but we were so keen to ensure the job was properly done that we both checked the lock two or three times, to make sure it was secure.

Selkman had been another matter entirely. He remained on the cold, wet ground outside the house, his enormous size and weight meaning that, even working together, Elizabeth and I were not able to carry or drag him into the house. The best we were able to do for the man was to cover him with two large, heavy, woollen blankets that Elizabeth brought down from her room, though I first made sure to bind Selkman's legs and arms so tightly that I may well have limited the circulation of his blood. But it was rather that than take the slightest risk of him breaking free from his bonds, should he come round while still bound.

However, both Elizabeth and I felt an immense degree of frustration at finding Sneijder had fled the property, most likely while I was fighting with the housekeeper, or perhaps after he had seen her knocked to the ground by Elizabeth. We both had a strong desire for revenge on the Doctor, more especially so Elizabeth, who shivered at the thought of how things might have turned out for her without my unexpected arrival. We searched the house from top to bottom, then much of the grounds, but there was no sign of the evil man. I supposed that he knew the lie of the land well enough to find his way to a railway station and from there, whatever direction he might take, there seemed little doubt he would ultimately seek to return to Germany. By the time we gave up our search, with great reluctance and frustration, we were both tired and hungry, so had made our way to the kitchen to help ourselves to some of the supplies from the impressively stocked larder.

My slab of bread and jam finally finished, I leaned back in my chair and wiped the crumbs from my lips as a sense of contentment and ease filled me for the first time in quite a while.

"What will we do now?" asked Elizabeth, placing her teacup on its saucer.

"I will have to go for help, I should say. It's a damned nuisance about this fog, which seems determined to cling to these hills for every minute it can manage, but Selkman and Rafferty will need to be taken into custody and the other patients will need some attending to, I should imagine."

"Mrs Downing seems to be in rather a bad way. She is so very confused and has asked several times if I know where Doctor Sneijder is. I do hope someone can reverse what that man has done to her."

"I would be surprised if there isn't some expert medical man in London who knows how to undo Sneijder's work. I should imagine he will be a busy man if the police can find some sort of list of all the other people that have had the misfortune to find themselves patients here."

"Will you be able to find your way in the fog? I don't imagine you know this part of the world very well and you won't be much of a help to the rest of us if you should get yourself lost on the hills."

"I'll stick to the road. Even if it takes me an hour or two, I'm bound to come across some cottage or farm eventually and, once I've found someone with local knowledge and a means of transport, it should be no problem to make my way to the nearest authorities. I only hope I can do so in time for them to apprehend Sneijder before he can put much distance between himself and this place."

Elizabeth looked outside and the same thought occurred

to her as had already hit me.

“There isn’t a great deal of light left. Would it not be better to set off tomorrow morning?”

“If not for Sneijder, I would no doubt do just that, but I wouldn’t get a great deal of sleep knowing that, with every hour that passed, he was making good his escape. No, I would say I have up to an hour of daylight remaining, at least enough in which to see. I suppose you had better leave the lights on in this place and all the curtains open in case I should need to find my way back, though I hope that is not necessary.”

We briefly discussed Elizabeth’s options should I have not returned by the morning, then I rose to my feet, pulled on my jacket and coat, along with a fur-lined hat we had found in the cloakroom, and exchanged farewells with Elizabeth. If she was at all disconcerted by my imminent departure, she did not for one minute let it show, but wished me luck and waved after me as I stepped out of the kitchen and into the growing gloom.

*

As the door closed behind me, I knew Elizabeth would be returning to the other patients, who were waiting for her in the sitting room, its furniture restored to some sort of order. They had been left playing cards, as best they could through the confusion in their minds. For me, there was a journey into the unknown in search of relief and rescue. As I stepped on to the road, I heard a seagull cry out somewhere overhead and, looking up, I saw, for the first time since that damned journey on the farm cart, a very definite break in the fog, the sky visible for a short while until the fog closed back up. I could do nothing other than take it as a good omen and my heart filled with joy and enthusiasm for the journey ahead, causing me to lengthen my stride, as much as I could without causing my ribs to complain.

I was fortunate that the road presented me with no choices, remaining a single, narrow thread, for I suspect I would have been entirely befuddled as to which way to go had I encountered a fork or junction. As I continued to walk, further breaks in the fog opened up, some of them closing all too quickly, but others remaining, growing even, so that I began to get a better view of the landscape and where I was heading. It seemed, in fact, that I was entirely surrounded by fields for the grazing of sheep.

After very nearly half an hour, I crested a short, shallow hill, where the road began to take a gentle swing to the left. As I looked down, I found the fog had shifted away almost entirely ahead of me and there, perhaps half a mile away, sitting on a short, exposed ridge of land, was a farm and visible in a window was a light, flickering but persistent. Drawing air deep into my lungs and starting on a little ditty to which I knew perhaps a quarter of the words, I set off with something approaching a spring in my step, the pain in my ribs overwhelmed, for the moment, by the happiness I now felt. At last, help was within my grasp.

THE LATE ARRIVAL

My godparents, John and Susan Buchan, were so delighted to see me finally arrive on their doorstep at Hillside House that my godmother couldn't stop tears from filling her eyes. The two of them had, of course, realised something was wrong, but their persistent efforts at making contact with me, or someone who could explain what had happened to me, had all come to nothing. Given the circumstances of my detour to Sneijder's house, that was entirely to be expected.

After being made a terrible fuss of by my godmother, the three of us sat down to afternoon tea on their fine terrace, overlooking the cut through which flowed the narrow, energetic stream that would, in a short distance, be referred to as the River Nith. The weather seemed keen to make up for those previous days of heavy, cold fog and the sun had been bright and warm all day. I took off my jacket and laid it on an empty chair.

I was, of course, required to provide my godparents with a full description of my adventure, leaving out none of the more distressing parts in consideration of my godmother, who has a considerable appetite for such stories. They were rather shocked to discover that it was possible for someone such as Sneijder to so distort the mind of a fellow human being that he could potentially turn them against their own countrymen. Given the ever-growing threat of war, it presented a very worrying situation, though one that I lacked the expertise to comment further on.

Having reached the part of my story where I had left Elizabeth Fitzsimon and the other patients waiting in the Doctor's house while I walked through the fog in search of help, I paused to take a sip of tea, which, I must admit, I lingered over a little more than was really necessary.

"Alex, darling, don't be such a tease," complained my godmother, poking a finger into my forearm. "We want to know what happened next, especially to that awful German Doctor."

"Well, I must say, the poor farmer on whose door I knocked seeking assistance took quite some persuading that I wasn't a complete lunatic. He made me wait on the doorstep for a good long while, holding the door half-closed, as I set the scene. It was only when I mentioned yourselves that his expression changed and he began to consider I might not be as mad as he feared."

"He knew of us then, I take it?" asked my godfather.

"By name, yes. After a little more effort, I was able to persuade him to at least go up to the Doctor's house with me and see for himself what the situation was. I must say, he wasn't keen, but, having spoken to his wife, he harnessed up a horse to his cart and off we went. He didn't say much on the way there, but once he'd seen for himself how things were and heard a word or two from Miss Fitzsimon, he changed his tune altogether and became quite free with his words."

"Thanks Heavens for that," chipped in my godmother, the excitement of my story clear to see in her bright, eager eyes.

"After that, he took me on to the railway station, where the station master, the one I met on my arrival, was able to put a call through to the police station in Kilmarnock. It caused quite the stir, by all accounts. A dozen officers were sent out at once from Glasgow to attend to Selkman and the housekeeper and, of course, to scour the hillsides for Sneijder."

I couldn't resist the temptation to once more add a little drama to the situation by pausing my tale as I sipped again at my cup of tea.

"Honestly, Alex, I'll have McAllister throw you in the stream in a minute if you don't stop stringing out your tale," insisted my godmother. "Did they catch the horrid man?"

"Well, it was by then late, you appreciate. Darkness had set in and it was a tricky business attempting to search for a man in the hills, but, yes, they found him, eventually. He was in rather a bad way, by all accounts. When he fled from the house, the fool had taken nothing more with him than his jacket and a hat, then he'd had the misfortune to fall into a small gulley not more than a quarter of a mile into his escape, breaking his leg as he fell. When the police found him, he was so desperate for assistance that he seemed not overly worried that he had fallen into the hands of the very authorities he had been hoping to evade."

"Thank the Lord for that," said my godmother, with a sigh of relief. "I couldn't stand to think that he might still be roaming about the hills while we were sleeping in our beds at night. Desperate men can do the most terrible things."

"I think if anyone attempted to break in here, my dear, then Charlemagne would soon see them off. He'd probably enjoy the chase," added my godfather, referring to their golden retriever, who had a notoriously bad temper when woken from his sleep.

"And what happened to those poor people who were

brought under the Doctor's spell?" asked my godmother.

"They are on their way up to Glasgow. The inspector in charge of the police party informed me they have some excellent medical people there who will be able to undo the damage."

"Did you get chance to say goodbye to that young lady, Miss Fitzsimon? She sounds like quite a feisty individual. Rather like me," added my godmother, with something of a sparkle in her eye.

"Yes, I'm pleased to say that I had the opportunity to wish her well. And you're right, without her help I wouldn't in all likelihood be sitting here now, telling you my little story. We all have a good deal to thank her for."

"So, what have they done with Sneijder?" asked my godfather, leaning back in his chair and looking over the top of his glasses, as he had a habit of doing when discussing a serious business. "Or did the police not care to say?"

"The inspector would only say that Sneijder would be taken to the main police station in Glasgow. The same was true for Selkman and the housekeeper, Rafferty. I'm not sure he actually knew what would happen after that. No doubt the authorities will send someone up from London to speak to Sneijder and the others to see what more they can find out."

"So, Selkman and the housekeeper had only been knocked unconscious, I take it?" asked my godfather, sounding as though he was almost disappointed they had not suffered a worse fate.

"They had and I'm pleased about that. I couldn't really say how I might cope with the knowledge I was responsible for taking another person's life. It can't be easy sleeping at night when you've done such a thing."

"Well, it's all a most disturbing situation," observed my godfather. "I imagine the police will have a heck of a time trying to track down all of Sneijder's other victims. If he's been up here a year practising his witchcraft, that will most likely amount to quite a considerable number of people."

"Hundreds, I should think," I observed. "And Lord knows what positions of influence they are in."

"It's been quite the adventure for you, then, my dear," smiled my godmother. "But you can't go expecting such a thing every time you travel up here to visit us, you know."

I laughed, more than was good for me, because it made my bruised ribs ache, despite the bandages that were now wrapped tightly around them. My godmother was absolutely right, I'd had a quite extraordinary adventure and certainly not the sort of thing that the average chap expects to experience during his life. One minute I was at Euston railway station, talking over old times with a school chum I hadn't seen in years, then the next I was locked up in a horrid cellar fearing for my life, then crashing a huge wooden hammer down on Selkman's head.

Looking back at things also made me realise just how fortunate I had been to come through it all in one piece. A little difference here or there and things might well have turned out very badly for me. It was a distinctly unsettling thought and one I pushed to the back of my mind almost as soon as it occurred to me.

From the back of the house came the sound of a dog barking and, as I looked round, I found myself confronted by an over-excited golden retriever that ran straight up to me in leaps and bounds, then lifted its front paws on to my lap, so it could set about licking my face. My mind was at once taken off all thoughts of my recent brush with death.

LONDON

I was standing by one of the large, panelled windows in my Pimlico flat, looking out over the little garden that occupied the centre of the square in which I lived. It was a glorious spring day, bright sunshine and only the merest hint of a cloud in the sky. The trees and shrubbery in the garden were covered with flawless, fresh leaves, in such a delightful shade of soft, velvet-like green that they looked almost man-made. An elderly couple, the gentleman aided by the use of a walking stick, were strolling through the garden, seemingly content to enjoy nature's beauty and, perhaps, to engage in a little conversation.

They would not, I felt sure, be discussing the recent events in Scotland that had so occupied my time, since, in the interests of national security, the Government had insisted the newspaper people not mention a word of it and, like all good Englishmen, they had abided by this prohibition. That rather suited me, as I was not the least bit keen on giving an account of myself to some over-eager reporter type, flourishing his notepad and badly-worn pencil. The limelight was most definitely not something I craved. No, I had other things on my mind. Rather pressing things, as it happened.

I had returned to London the day before, after spending two delightful days with my godparents, who had, once again, spoiled me terribly. After my narrow escape from the claws of Sneijder, my godmother had been utterly desperate to shower me with every little luxury she could conjure up, perhaps worried I might find myself in a similar situation on my return journey and, on this occasion, fail to escape with my life. It was a blow to have to leave them when the time came, but London and my job called, so I left them on the platform at Glasgow station, my godmother having insisted they accompany me that far, from where I caught the night train back south. Of course, I was obliged to inform them of my safe arrival the very second I set foot on the ground at Euston station.

There had been but one thing, other than Sneijder and his co-conspirators, that had occupied my thoughts on the train during the journey south and that was my utter determination to be married to Caroline at the earliest opportunity, should she be willing to have me, of course. My brush with death had made me see how things might be suddenly taken away from a person and left me with a clear picture that I should not delay seizing such momentous and joyous opportunities for any longer than I absolutely needed to. I also decided it would be a very good thing to spend a little more time with my parents, whom I had, in recent years, visited shamefully infrequently, although they were far too loving to ever say anything of the sort to me.

Thus, on the very afternoon of my arrival back in London, having first washed and changed into some clean clothing at my flat, I made my way across town to the Carsons' family home, sought and obtained consent from Caroline's father to marry his eldest daughter, then made my nervous proposal to Caroline in the privacy of the small garden at the back of their house. I must admit, I think I was rather more nervous than I had been while looking down the barrel of that revolver in Scotland, but I dropped to one knee and made my plea to my darling Caroline.

She is a terrible tease sometimes, my fiancée, and she dithered a little too long for comfort before she put me out of my misery and said yes, practically knocking me off my feet when she threw herself at me in celebration. I do believe half of London already knows about the engagement. Of course, my decision being such an impulsive one, I did not have a ring to give her, but she was not put off by such an oversight and assured me we would soon make a visit to Hatton Garden in search of something suitably expensive. For a while, I feared I would become a bankrupt even before we reached the wedding day.

But my business in London at that time was not all concerned with marriage proposals and weddings. On the morning of my second day back, I had received a visitor to my flat, a round-faced man, with an entirely bald head and extravagantly large eyebrows, in which could have nested a wren or two. I thought at first that he was one of those pedlars of life insurance policies who go door to door, hoping to tempt some poor soul into parting with a sizeable sum of money in return for very little by way of benefit. Indeed, I had all but slammed the door shut on him when, in a quiet, firm voice, he mentioned the name Sneijder, at which I stopped and stared at him in a state of mild shock. How, I wondered, could he possibly know that name? For a moment, I feared he might be some sort of conspirator of the Doctor's, come to exact a terrible revenge, but as I hesitated, the bald man pushed his way in and sat himself down in my sitting room.

"Who are you?" I demanded, rather confounded by his lack of good manners.

"You don't need to know my name," he replied,

speaking with a distinct Welsh accent, soft and melodic. “Only that I represent His Majesty’s Government.”

“You mentioned a name just now.”

“Sneijder?”

“That’s the one. I don’t suppose that was a coincidence?”

“Would you believe me if I claimed it was?”

“No.” There was a pause as I eyed the fellow up. His suit looked a little cheap, but his shoes were well polished and his nails clean and clipped. I had met a good many people involved in the government of the Empire during the course of my work and this man sitting before me appeared as good a match as any. “What do you know of Sneijder?”

He looked at me from under those bushy dark brows, as if he was, in turn, weighing me up, something I found a little disturbing. “A German Doctor who has been busy planting dangerous false notions in the minds of British citizens, operating from a house in Scotland.”

“I hope you’re not about to tell me he’s managed to escape.”

“I very much doubt that Doctor Sneijder is going to get a chance to escape, not where he’s locked up. No, Mr Templeman, I am here on a related matter.”

“Mm,” I was keen on finding out what the man had to say for himself, but, for the time being, I was even more keen to hear what had happened to Sneijder since I had left Scotland and this man sitting in front of me might very well be my only opportunity to find out. “Before we get on to your agenda, I’d appreciate you explaining to me what has become of Sneijder and his fellow conspirators since their arrest.”

I sat down on the small, two-seater sofa opposite my guest and made it clear from my attitude that there would be no further conversation until he had met my request.

“That’s fair enough, I suppose.”

He dragged a handkerchief from out of a jacket pocket and blew his nose loudly before continuing. It did occur to me that he might have been giving himself some little time to decide just what he was and was not prepared to share with me, but I cared not, as long as I got a clear statement of events since Sneijder's arrest.

"Well," he went on, at length. "Following their arrest, Sneijder and his associates were brought down here to London, then shipped out to a high security prison on Dartmoor. Our best police officers and others," there was a momentary pause at this point, as if my visitor wanted to underline his reference to these 'other' people, "have been interrogating them since then. None of the three have turned out to be the talkative sort, more's the pity."

"So, you're telling me that the police have yet to learn anything useful from them?"

"That's the long and short of it, yes. But that's not been our only line of investigation. Excellent records were found at the house in Scotland, including details of all the victims, and specially selected police officers have been interviewing these people and one or two of their relatives."

He stopped to scratch at the side of one eye and as he did so he noticed a photograph of Caroline on the sideboard. He stared at it for a moment.

"Sister of yours?"

"No, actually it's my fiancée. I proposed to her yesterday, as it happens. After the recent events in Scotland, I decided I really ought to get on with things, before it was too late."

"Very sensible. Now then, back to our little story. It turns out that Sneijder had a handful of other people strategically placed around the country. Their job has been to befriend people in positions of influence, identify a family member who could be suggested to have some sort of mental problem, then step in with a helpful suggestion to the relative that they ought to arrange for a consultation with the marvellous Doctor Sneijder. It's unlikely everyone took up the offer, of course, but plenty did and certainly enough to matter. A well-thought-out scheme, which would have been tricky to spot, if not for what happened to you."

"Do you know who all these accomplices are?"

"Happily we do. Sneijder made the mistake of keeping names and addresses in a folder at the house in Scotland. We've been busy over the last two days paying some unannounced house calls. There's only been one that's got away so far. A fellow who saw our men breaking into his property as he was returning home from a visit to the theatre. But don't worry, we'll catch up with him soon enough."

I scratched at the side of my head as I took in what I had been told, rather taken aback at the scale of the operation Sneijder had been running. It certainly wasn't an amateur scheme.

"That's quite remarkable. Has this sort of thing been done before?"

"Nothing quite the same as Sneijder's been doing. We're more used to your run-of-the-mill spying, trying to gain influence through friendship and blackmail, and attempts at stealing sensitive information. I suppose, though, we'll have to get used to schemes like this being tried. If it can be done once then it can be done again."

"There's a thought and not a pleasant one." Then something occurred to me that I really ought to have considered before. "But I don't suppose you have called on me today just to provide me with an update on your progress."

"Very perceptive of you, Mr Templeman. Indeed, that is not the reason I'm here today." My visitor shifted in his chair, as if preparing himself for some significant announcement. For a moment, I thought perhaps I ought not to have asked the question, least the result was something I didn't much like. "His Majesty's Government is always on the look-out for suitable people to employ, especially in… very specialised roles. The sort of thing that needs a cool head under pressure and an ability to think on your feet. Needs to be someone who can sort things out for themselves, when there's no one else around to give instructions or directions."

There was a look of expectation on his face, as if he believed he'd said more than enough to make himself crystal clear. In matter of fact, I didn't have the foggiest idea what he was talking about and I suppose he must have noticed the confusion in my expression, which I fear was rather clueless.

"We need people of our own to hunt down and root out dangerous men like Sneijder. They're always out there, trying to undermine the Empire. All the more so right now. And I take it I don't need to say anything further as to why that might be the case. The right sort are few and far between and my superiors and I are of the opinion you're just such a man. What you did up there in Scotland has impressed all the right people. Quite excited, some of them are."

I couldn't stop my eyebrows from flicking upwards at the surprise of what I'd just been told and I tried to cover up my confusion by leaning back in my chair and bringing my hands together on my lap as if in serious contemplation. After a moment or two, I fashioned a reply, of sorts, though it was a little hard not to laugh, so ridiculous did I consider the proposal.

"You mean, you're asking me if I'd like to become a spy?"

"The word 'spy' isn't something we like to use. It's more the sort of thing you get in an adventure story, not the serious business of protecting one's country. But that's the general idea, yes. It's not the sort of offer we make every day of the week. Only the very best candidates get approached. It's quite a privilege."

I paused, a sliver of a smile on my face. It seemed I had let into my house a salesman of sorts after all. The fellow appeared rather keen to complete the deal and was already doing a good deal to persuade me to sign up. But it was so out of the blue I found myself almost at once dreaming up a thousand questions, not the least of which was how on earth I would explain such a development to Caroline. Or perhaps the idea was not to say anything at all. Yes, I was flattered, I'll admit it, but I was also hesitant and confused.

"Well… Of course, I'm keen to help my country, but… as I mentioned, I'm to be married soon and there, no doubt, there will be children. It's a lot to consider."

No doubt my guest had received such an uncertain response on previous occasions he'd made such a proposal to a prospective spy, since he appeared not the least put out by my reticence; not a trace of disappointment or surprise on his face.

"You don't need to make up your mind today, Mr Templeman. You'll be wanting to think it over. Most people do, not that we ask very many, of course. We run a well-oiled machine, let me say that much. You'll get some excellent training to help you along the way and one of our more experienced men will guide you through your first year or so. You don't need to worry about being dropped in the deep end and left to drown."

"I see. Good."

"Well, you think it over," suggested my guest, before rising to his feet and doing up his jacket. "I'll be back in two days' time for an answer."

"Two days."

I climbed to my feet, still somewhat in a daze, and escorted my visitor to the front door.

"Oh and one more thing," he said as he placed his hat back on his head. "Best not say anything to that fiancée of yours, or anyone else for that matter. Need to keep these things hush-hush, I'm sure you understand."

"Yes, Of course."

I closed the door behind him before returning to my chair, where I sat in silence for almost an hour, confounded and confused by such an unexpected development.

It was a state of mind that had not altogether left me as I rose to my feet and took up station by a window, from where I was able to look out at the park. A middle-aged couple were taking a stroll but I was not at all in the frame of mind to pay them any attention, since I was pre-occupied with the notion that I could, if I so chose, take up the profession of spy. But how to make a decision?

Of one thing I was absolutely certain; prior to the recent events in Scotland, I would not even have considered myself suitable material for any such undertaking. Indeed, I had considered myself really a rather unadventurous and unremarkable sort of fellow. I knew I was the determined sort and quick to adapt to a new situation, but that's a long way from fighting with enemy spies on a lonely, fog-bound Scottish hillside.

As I gave thought to the unexpected proposal, I begun to see that perhaps I had never given myself sufficient credit for my abilities, not being the kind of person to blow his own trumpet and all that. Maybe I had more about me than I had realised. After all, the odds had been tremendously against me in Scotland and yet I had made it through. It certainly would bring me a life of adventure and excitement if I was to accept and there was, of course, the looming threat of war, when we would all need to put our shoulder to the wheel.

On the other hand, I was about to become a married man and my work, unexciting and often boring as it was, did provide a steady income and one sufficient on which to raise a family. It was a great deal to give up. I found myself deeply regretting not being able to consult Caroline on the matter, for I was sure she would be of considerable help in clearing my mind.

I looked again out the window. The couple walking in the park made their way through the gate on the far side, leaving the trees and shrubbery entirely to the birds. Several of these flew down on to the lawn, where they set about searching for morsels to eat. A Hackney carriage turned in at the top of the square and made its way along the road to a house on the far side, where a woman in a delightful summer dress stepped out on to the pavement before entering the house. For one brief moment I thought it might be Elizabeth Fitzsimon, her blonde hair so similar in tone and form, but she was someone else entirely.

My thoughts returned to Scotland. It had been quite a considerable adventure and I wasn't sure I wanted it to be the only one of the sort that I experienced in my lifetime. It seemed I had an answer for my visitor when he returned.

* * * The End * * *

Alexander Templeman will return in a new story.

FREE Book by Ben Westerham

You can also subscribe to Ben's newsletter for information on discounted offers, new releases, competitions, plus free and exclusive stories and bonus material. You also get a free ebook copy of one of Ben's novels by way of a welcome gift.

Find out more here
http://www.benwesterham.com/landing-page

If you enjoyed this book then please consider posting a review.

Many thanks,

Ben Westerham

From the Banbury Cross Murder Mystery series

From 'The Hide and Seek Murders'

Eleanor Golightly never saw so much as a glimpse of the figure that moved up behind her, swift and silent, from the cover of the shrubbery. Indeed, she was only very briefly aware of the immense blow that came crashing down on her head. Just for a second or two, the world seemed to stop in silence, a peculiar sensation that she couldn't quite get to grips with before it had passed and she collapsed on to the immaculately cut lawn.

From 'The Club of Death'

Henry Graball was aglow with the flush of success. Hardly a novel experience to him, but a most satisfying one all the same. The room he surveyed from his vantage point at the bar was packed with the great and good of Banbury, every single invitation he'd issued having received a positive response. Hardly surprising, he reminded himself, since none of the hopeless, toadying bunch would have dared to risk turning him down. They'd be far too afraid of upsetting him. And there were very few people indeed who could afford to do such a thing.

From the David Good private investigator series

From 'Good Investigations'

"Mr Good," she purred like a hungry cat meeting a blind mouse, "and I do hope you will be." She slid beautifully, effortlessly in to the knackered old punter's chair, and I swear the thing wrapped itself lovingly around her sexy, lithe frame. Then she tempted me with those dark bewitching eyes, calling me closer, closer, closer

From 'Good Girl Gone Bad'

If you ask me, good girls can be the baddest there are, if the fancy takes them. Maybe it's because they save it all up for one big splurge, then go mad bad. I don't know, but what I do know is that anyone who tries telling you some little darling of theirs' wouldn't say boo to a goose is either stupid, misinformed or both. Any goody two shoes type should carry a health warning, 'Danger, Good Girl. May go bad at any moment'.

You can find out more about Ben Westerham at
www.benwesterham.com.

Printed in Great Britain
by Amazon

36691615R00096